I LOVE HIM, HE LOVES ME NOT

Literati Media Group

ISBN 978-0-9895223-0-4

Printed in the United States of America

*All characters, events, establishments, and organizations mentioned in this book are a complete work of fiction. Any similarities to any person, either living or deceased, are both coincidental and unintentional.

Cover Art Provided by:
Lauren M. Biggs
biggs_l@yahoo.com

Content Edited by:
Sabrina Smith-Dalrymple
yourwordsmyeyes@gmail.com

Media Content provided by:
Bruce A. Lucas
LiteratiMediaGroup@gmail.com

ACKNOWLEDGMENTS

I have loved, hated, and then loved this novel for the last year or so. I have put my all into it, and then pulled back more than a dozen times. I've been confident about the storyline, sure of my decisions on how it should go, and then trashed it all, feeling it wasn't worth it or good enough. I only have one thing to say to all the people who stood by it, confirmed my feelings on it, and made me push to complete it: **THANK YOU FOR BEING WITH ME THROUGH IT ALL!**

First, thank you, God. This crazy, mixed-up mind belongs to you. I praise you with everything I am. I hope your light shines bright enough through me that no one ever wonders if Christ is in my life. Thank you for my gifts. Thank you for my talents. I owe it all to you.

Thank you, Mom and Dad. You've given me permission to be who I am. Bruce, Lani, and Cherie... my big bro, and the baby sisters, ya'll already know what's up. Apparently, we were meant to be each other's support system. Thank you for letting me bounce ideas off of you and call you at all times of the day about my silly ramblings. The conversations— even if they weren't about anything in particular, helped me seed through my internal chaos to create this book. Once again, you've come through in ways only you all could understand.

To the team of Literati (Literati Media Group), we are off to a great start. It took us a year, but we are standing on a strong foundation that we've built together. Lauren, thank you for your artistic creativity. My book cover is all that I hoped it would be. Bruce, I have no idea what I'm doing, but you understand exactly how I want my book trailers to look. Kenny, a.k.a. "Mr. Persuasion". You're going to keep us relevant. Arielle... it started at the Piccadilly. Remember that when we are big and famous.

To all of the supporters of my work, I say thank you, may God bless you, and I love you.

Dedicated to the memory of my Grandmothers, Lelia Malone, & Lena Mosby; two women who never wanted for any man.

Rest in peace, ladies
1927 - 2013

I LOVE HIM, HE LOVES ME NOT

"Now babies… you've both been very naughty girls. You're punishment will be severe for all of the bad things you have done." Valley gave her doll baby's a very stern look as she paced the floor in front of them. It was Saturday afternoon tea, and it was rudely interrupted when Baby Wet-Wet had an accident that created a puddle of fake urine under her seat as they sat around Valley's play kitchen table for their afternoon crumpets and a spot of English tea. Her other guest, Dolly Surprise would have been saved from the punishment, had she not been an accomplice by keeping her mouth shut when Baby Wet-Wet made a mess.

"Doing bad things will not be tolerated." Valley folded her arms as she reprimanded her babies. "You know how much it pains me to punish you both, but what has to be done, has to be done." Valley stood in front of her inanimate dolls as if waiting for their response. As expected, their painted-on eyes stared blankly at Valley while she lectured them on proper decorum during tea time.

"Dolly, because you didn't speak up about what Baby Wet-Wet did, you will have to be punished first." Valley grabbed her doll baby's hair and was just about to yank it hard enough to pop her head off when she heard the stern voice of her mother calling her name.

"Valley! Come here, right away!" Shaundra yelled up the stairs to Valley; irritated that her child had disrespected her once again by not keeping up with her regular chores.

"Yes mother! I'm coming right away!" Not knowing exactly what her mother wanted, Valley understood the tone of her voice meant she had done something to displease her. "Dolly, you are not off the hook. I will deal with you when I return." Valley dropped Dolly Surprise without delay because she knew if she took too much time responding to her mother's request; the punishment would be more severe than already planned.

Valley's footsteps could be heard as she ran down the stairs. She paused at the bottom of them to smooth out any unsightly wrinkles in the dress her mother meticulously handpicked from her closet full of clothes fit for a princess. She then took a deep breath, and calmly walked into the kitchen where her mother and father were... dad at the table reading his news paper, and mommy at the sink irritated; tapping just one finger and just one foot.

"Valley... what did you do? Mommy looks upset."

"I didn't do anything. I was a good girl today." Valley spoke to the voices inside of her who kept a watchful eye. They were useful in keeping her on the straight and narrow, but they were also notorious in getting her in worlds of terrible trouble.

Valley stood at attention and scanned the room for her offending act but saw nothing out of place. However, her brow began to glisten from the beads of nervous sweat that had begun to form from anxiousness.

"Valley, think of something quick! You're gonna get it for sure!"

She looked helplessly at her father in hopes that he could give her a hint of what was to come, but he continued to remain engrossed in the sports section of the Richmond Times Dispatch. Unfortunately, Valley had no choice but to call her attention to her mother, who waited patiently for her child to grant her the undivided attention she so rightly deserved.

Without one word, Shaundra turned to the sink and pulled out a dirty plate, one fork, and an unwashed cup.

Valley noticed those utensils as her own. She turned beet red from embarrassment because she was about to be punished over a petty crime that she could have easily avoided.

"Ooooh, Valley! Look what you did! This is very bad!"

"Oh mom... thanks for bringing that to my attention. I was going to wash those dishes after dad finished his breakfast."

Shaundra didn't react to Valley's feeble attempt to correct her mishap. For dramatics, she purposely let the dishes fall back into the sink with no regard, and they slammed and clanked into each other as they hit the stainless steel pit.

"Get ready Valley, and say a prayer 'cause only God forgives."

"Be quiet. Mommy might hear us and get madder." The voices in her head agreed with her command, and settled down and became still. They feared mommy just as much as Valley did, and hated the punishments just as much.

Shaundra silently walked to the utility closet and came back with a brown, quarter of an inch thick worn out leather belt. She nodded her head down and looked at Valley from beneath her wrinkled brow, and uttered one word.

"Strip."

Shaking like a leaf, Valley knew there was no excuse good enough when her mother had made her mind up to carry out the punishment. She looked over at her dad hoping to make one last attempt for help. He didn't budge from the sports section, but turned the page unceremoniously to read the next headline; never having acknowledged her presence, even though he knew what she'd have to endure.

"Dad... are you finished with your breakfast? I can take that for you." Valley made a meager attempt to right her wrong. Instead of answering her, Jack made a coughing noise, but still kept his head in his paper trying to stay uninvolved.

There was no use. She regretfully had to prepare for her beating. Valley slowly unbuttoned the back of her dress, and hesitantly shoved the sleeves off her bare shoulders to let the dress drop to the floor. She then unbuckled her patent leather Mary Jane's and kicked them off her feet. She rolled her socks off and placed one in each shoe. She took off her starch white panties, gathered up her dress, under garments, and her shoes and placed them neatly on the dining room table. Valley walked solemnly back into the kitchen— scared but showing no fear. Her mother was a stickler for being neat and tidy, and Valley learned the hard way that a dirty house was an unruly house that needed to be controlled.

"I'm ready." One tear trickled out of Valley's left eye. She huffed her bare chest outward proudly like a warrior preparing for death.

"Very Well." Shaundra spoke the words signaling the beginning of the punishment ritual.

Shaundra could admit to herself that the punishments were harsh, but her dirty little secret was that she was very aware of Valley's demented behavior. Dr. Sumpter warned her that Valley was different and needed specific care, but she wouldn't listen. She'd let her pride control her decision to raise Valley the way she saw fit, and what she learned from her mistake was that Valley was sneaky when it came to her devious acts. Unfortunately for Valley, Shaundra knew about the things her daughter kept hidden. She knew about the scary drawings Valley kept underneath her bed. She knew about the scratched up pictures of her that Valley crumpled up and stuffed in her drawers. She also knew about how much Valley adored Jack more than she liked her own mother (that hurt the most). The punishments Shaundra dealt out paid for all of Valley's transgressions. In a way, it was easier to deal with her bad behavior in the privacy of their own home, than the rigorous routine of doctor appointments, the medicine, and the total humiliation she felt having to explain her child to her friends with perfectly normal children.

Shaundra watched as Valley placed her feet on the plush red towel that sat folded on the floor, and then she placed her hands on the counter to brace herself. Shaundra then filled a cup up with cold water from the faucet, and poured it onto Valley's naked skin.

Valley felt the goose bumps rise on her arms and back as the water raced down her body. She shut her eyes as she sensed her mother's hand drawing back with belt in hand.

The brown belt hit Valley's young supple back. Her soaked skin made the sting of her punishment hurt worse. She tightened her eyes as she felt the pain all over. The belt went up in the air once again and came back down, striking her in the same place; making her arch her back and her head lift upward to the sky, but she wouldn't cry out in pain. If Valley let out the slightest hint of agony, it would set her mother in a frenzy. Shaundra never liked when Valley cried while getting a spanking. The rule was if you got in trouble for something you did, you weren't allowed to cry about it— you were expected to take your punishment with honor and dignity.

Another crack from the belt across her bare backside... the tender spot. The sting became a heated tingle, but the pain was still prominent. Her knees buckled, but her hands that were braced on the counter, caught her from falling out in pain. Shaundra's limit on delivering lashes was four. There was only one more left.

The last and final lash wrapped around her skinny legs as it struck her. Valley could feel the leather belt slide off of her as Shaundra retracted it.

Finally, the punishment was over.

The room was silent. Shaundra stood looking at Valley who held all her pain inside. Valley's little body convulsed slightly as she recovered from the ordeal. Shaundra didn't like striking her child, but punishments kept Valley from getting out of control. She tilted her head towards the dining room as a signal to Valley that it was now okay for her to retrieve her clothes.

Valley walked back into the dining room, scooped up her things, and got dressed while her mother watched on without emotion. More composed, Valley put her shoes back on and walked over to her mother and gave her a heartfelt hug.

"Sorry mommy. I didn't mean to make you punish me. Please forgive me for leaving dirty dishes in the sink."

Shaundra stood with hand on her hip while Valley hugged her; never returning the sentiment of affection. It was all part of the routine— acknowledge, punish, redemption.

"You are forgiven." Shaundra stated in a lack-luster tone.

Valley's father put the sports section down; coincidently finished reading the stimulating articles about the games from the week and what sporting events were scheduled for the following.

"Well my darling, Valley Girl. Would you like to go out for ice cream? I bet you'd like a banana split topped with sprinkles, and chocolate syrup."

Jack smiled at his precious daughter, and then wrapped her in his arms careful not to squeeze too tight. Valley's father was a coward, but she didn't care. He was all she had left. She put on her smile, and allowed herself to feel some kind of appreciation for him as though he'd done all he could to stop Shaundra from punishing her.

"Yeah! I'll go get my coat!" Valley said as cheerfully as she could.

Valley made her way to her room. The pain from her punishment was still with her. As she grabbed her cardigan she caught a glimpse of herself in the mirror. There wasn't a hint of the emotional or physical beating she'd just received. She clinched her sweater tightly in her hands as she thought about how much she hated her mother.

CHAPTER ONE

Pain…. Peace… thy soul departs.
Rough… hurt…. loss… danger.
I love him, but he doesn't know.
However, he knows that I do.

I'm inside…deep… deeper…deepest.
Further than I've ever been.
I'm in the darkest corner inside my mind thinking of him.
Breathing hard… soft… gasping. Hands grasping… choking…me.
Choking him.

I love him.

(He hurts me because I hurt myself.)

He loves me not.

He doesn't know.
(But he will know.)

"I wrote that poem for him. How do you like it?"

"It's umm… passionate. Very strong words… 'rough, choke, pain…'
What message were you trying to convey? What were you trying to
tell him?"

"About my love, and that the love I have for him is so deep and strong that we are intertwined. We are together because of the love I feel.

"I see..."

"No you don't see. You don't see what I've done for him. You don't see that I have made him into a better person. My love has changed him. You don't see that. All you see is the blood— the loss of his blood. You see what everyone else sees and not what I see. You say you see, but you see with other eyes and not with mine. See with my eyes Doctor Sumpter. See what I have done for him and then you'll understand."

"From all that you have said over the time we've worked together, the young man you speak of was very special to you. This love you believe you felt compelled you to end someone's life—"

"Now, wait a minute Doc! I wasn't the one who took his life! I-DID-NOT-TAKE-HIS-LIFE! I saved him from himself and that crazy bitch! She was the one who took his life! I released him from the inside out so that we could be as one in peace! We live happy together now because I saved him! And when I leave here, I'm going home to cook him some dinner. And when he finishes eating that delicious meal, I'm going to fuck his brains out!"

Valley was livid and feeling out of her skin when the Doctor spoke the wicked untruth about her fiancé. The deplorable words that were spat from his lips put Valley out of the chair facing him, and his insensitivity towards her tragedy made her pace the floor in a racing panic. No one understood that Ramses would always and forever be her lover, and she never liked anyone disrespecting their relationship.

Watching her erratic behavior, Dr. Sumpter became distressed by his patient's outrage over the man she claims was killed by the hands of another woman. He'd been working with his patient, Valley, to get her to understand the events that led up to the faithful day when she put a blade to the accused woman's neck in an act of retribution. But ever since Valley was arrested, she was under the illusion that she was in fact a hero.

Per the request of the State of Virginia, Valley Rain De'Amore, a twenty year old runaway had been in his care for the past six months helping her decipher what was real and what wasn't. Dr. Sumpter deemed it best she be scheduled for once a week one hour sessions in a small room with no windows; where a clear, heavy-duty partition separated him from his client. Valley was dangerous to herself and to others, but from the looks of her long stringy red hair, pale freckled skin, and her apple green colored eyes, no one would suspect a killer dwelled within her. However, the file on her psychological makeup told a different story.

Dr. Sumpter rubbed the bridge of his nose under his thick rimmed glasses before he flipped the legal pad to a clean sheet of paper. "Let's switch modes for a moment. Let's revisit the topic of your parents. Last time we spoke, we touched on your relationship with them. Let's go back and explore those feelings once again."

Before Dr. Sumpter mentioned her parents, Valley was plotting out ways to kill the ignorant bastard psychiatrist for his tactless comments, but all that changed when he asked her to discuss her parents. Her parents were a soft spot. She loved her mom and dad and wanted the Doctor to know about them. She paused her pacing in mid step and happily skipped back to her seat with a big toothy smile spread across her face.

"Oh Doctor! I would love to talk about them!" Valley sat back down in her seat and crossed her hands on top of the table that held her cup of water and a box of tissues. The remnants of the little girl she once was showed throughout as she reminisced about her wonderful parents.

"They are such good parents, Doc. Mommy and daddy are so wonderful to me. Do you know my mommy braids my hair every morning before I go to school and daddy walks me to my bus stop up the road? He likes to hold my lunch while we walk because I sometimes steal one of the cookies mommy packs for me. You know what?! I made all A's on my report card and daddy said I can get a puppy! I can't wait! I've wanted a puppy for a really, really long time."

"Yes, they are very nice people, and you are very lucky to have them." Dr. Sumpter scribbled some notes on his pad about Valley's drastic change in behavior and how she had once again reverted to her childhood when the topic of her parents came up.

"Valley, have your parents ever talked to you about where you came from?"

"Dr. Sumpter!" Valley said with a giggle. "I know where I came from! Mommy told me a long time ago that I came from where all babies come from!" Valley leaned back in her chair and slightly gapped her legs. She pointed to the space between them and then quickly put her hands to her mouth in embarrassment.

"Are you saying your mother give birth to you?"

"Ah-huh. Mommy and daddy made me just like all the other kids that came from their mommy's and daddy's. 'Cept... I don't look like my mommy, and all the other kids look like their mommies."

"Well, do you think you look like your father?"

"Nope." Valley shook her head vigorously from side to side as little girls do; letting her hair whip past her face in swayful movement. "I don't look like either one of them. Mommy has brown, curly, bushy hair, and brown skin, and daddy is the same color as me but his hair is yellow and wavy. I asked mommy why we all look so different from each other. She says that we are all the same on the inside, and what we look like on the outside doesn't matter. She says that we all come from the same place too... our mother's womb."

"Valley, do you understand what adoption is?"

"I think I do... I think adoption is when you pick out your kid at a store. I sometimes think mommy and daddy picked me out because we don't look alike."

"Have they ever told you, you were adopted?"

"I don't think so. I don't remember."

"What do you recall in reference to being with your parents?"

Valley screwed her mouth up in a tight ball as she thought hard about her parents. She closed her eyes and scratched her head as she pondered the Doctor's question even harder. A few seconds later, her eyes popped open when she remembered something from earlier in her childhood.

"I remember this one time mommy and daddy took me to a doctor. He wasn't a doctor like you, but he gave me a lollipop. I remember him telling mommy and daddy that the medicine will help me, but mommy and daddy told the nice man that I didn't need it, and all I needed was a good life and good friends and family that love me."

Dr. Sumpter paused as she spoke of the memory. He ignored the sensation to tear up as he heard her speak of thoughts he assumed were lost. Instead, he scribbled more notes in his pad and then checked his watch. "Valley, we have a few more minutes before the end of our session. Is there anything else you would like to tell me before I go for the day?"

"Ask him Valley... Ask him when we can leave."

Something the Doctor said in those last moments triggered her "switch" in attitude. Her demeanor was nothing like the little five year old girl persona that spoke of her parents so fondly just a short while ago. Nor was she like the violently crazed woman who stood accused and ready to attack when their session had begun. Now, Valley stared at the doctor blankly and began to speak in a listless monotone voice. "They want to know when am I getting the hell out of here. I have to get home."

"I'm sorry Valley. I can't authorize your release right now."

"See! I knew he wasn't going to let us out! She must still be out there looking for us!"

The thought of being hunted like a fox in old English sport sprang into Valley's head, and as suddenly as her face changed from the sweet little girl, to a woman staring blankly in the doctor's direction, her expression changed once again to a slight look of paranoia as she continued her conversation.

"Are you all keeping me here because his murderer is still free? The voices told me she's still looking to harm me." Valley let her hands rub over each other repeatedly as she looked around the room remembering that unforgettable day she almost died. She always got nervous when she thought about how the police saved her in the nick of time. It was frightening to hear that Ramses' killer lurked through Richmond in search of Valley because she hated them being together. In the midst of a crowded park, Sherry Vaughn boldly tried to slit Valley's throat for the sake of love. Valley thought her life was over as well when Ramses' killer had Valley cornered with nowhere to go.

"No Valley. We're keeping you here because you are not well. Once you are better, we will consider your release."

"Okay Doctor… I understand." Valley nodded her head in agreement, and watched as he walked out of the room. "I'm not well. I'll stay a little longer." Valley mumbled the Doctor's orders repeatedly to reassure herself.

Dr. Sumpter picked up his bag and headed to the door on his side of the room. He punched the buzzer and a guard came to relieve him of his duties, and another guard opened the door for Valley to be escorted back to her cell.

"Bye Doc. I'll stay in the hospital until I get better just like you said."

Dr. Sumpter gave Valley a hapless wave as he continued in the opposite direction of his patient.

As Valley walked down the hall back to her room, she hummed a melodic song. It was the same one her mother used to sing every time Valley had a bad day in school. While her mother sang the words of the soothing tune, she would give Valley a big hug to calm her little one down. Valley was no stranger to trouble due to her sadistic temper. Over the years, Valley would hum that tune when she wanted to feel that calm feeling once more. She hadn't hummed it in a long time, but as she walked down the hall, she felt it was the perfect time to do so.

CHAPTER Two

Dr. Sumpter stopped at the ward's exit to watch his patient make her way down the hall to her quiet cell. He shook his head in empathy as he looked at the pathetic sight. It was sad to know that her behavior could have been prevented had her parents taken her sickness more seriously. Once he saw the door to her room close, he continued the walk to his office to transfer the notes from his note pad to his laptop. When he got there, he sat behind his desk; exhausted from his hour session with the troubled young lady. He rubbed the space between his eyes once more before getting to work on the tedious task.

It was very well known around the hospital that this wasn't Dr. Sumpter's first time treating Valley. He remembered her as a little girl coming to him for meetings when she lived in a small town near South Boston. Back then, Valley was still a ward of the state with hopes of being adopted. It was a long road full of trial and error, but Dr. Sumpter changed a shy and depressed child into a happy well adjusted adolescent through intensive therapy and speculative treatment. As a rule, Dr. Sumpter never wanted to get too close to his patients, but he made an exception for Valley due to the extreme consequences of her particular case. In some ways, she was like one of his own children; being that he was her only father figure in some sense of the matter. Unlike his children, her tenth birthday was the last time he would see her. Valley had finally gotten adopted and her new parents were kind enough to bring her to his office for one last visit, and a slice of cake for him and Valley to split.

"Valley, I'm so happy for you." Dr. Sumpter took a sliver of the chocolate cake and placed it in his mouth. "You've grown into such a wonderful little lady. Your new parents seem like they are the perfect choice."

"Thank you Doctor Sumpter. I've waited for this day for so long. I can't believe it's finally here, and they're so nice too!" Valley took another bite of her cake as she grinned at the friendly man. "Do you know what? Mrs. Shaundra and Mr. Jack... oops..." Valley covered up her blunder with a giggle before she continued. "I mean mommy and daddy bought a new house, and we're moving there tomorrow. It's bigger than the one they have now, so I can have my own room. I've never had my own room before!"

"That's wonderful Valley!" Dr. Sumpter put his fork down and gave her a hug. "So what part of town will you be moving?"

"We're moving out of town... to Richmond! Mommy says we can all start new 'cause daddy got a job there. He's going to be a lawyer, and mommy is going to be an art teacher. They say since we are going to start new, I can be anything I want to be when we get to the big city. I think I want to be a ballerina!" Valley bounced in the chair with excitement about the big news. She couldn't wait to get on the road to the new house and her new adventure. She didn't have any friends at the foster home where she'd been living, and the kids at school picked on her mercilessly. Plus, there was also the accident Jeffery Turnbuckle had which everyone thought she had something to do with. Leaving all of that behind was the only thing she could think about.

The news of Valley's move gave Dr. Sumpter a shock. He wasn't prepared for the announcement, and he also wondered why Valley's parents never mentioned it before. He cleared his throat before he continued his conversation. "Valley, that's wonderful news. Starting over is a great idea." Dr. Sumpter stood up while he wiped the cake crumbs that had fallen on his shirt onto the hardwood floor. "Would you excuse me for a moment Valley? I would like to have a word with your parents."

"No problem Doc. You better hurry up though if you want to help me finish this piece of cake." Valley gave the doctor a big smile and made a fun chomping motion at it.

"You go ahead and finish it. I think I'm full." Dr. Sumpter patted his stomach while letting out a chuckle before he went to the waiting room to have a word with Shaundra and Jack. He pulled the door that separated his office from the waiting room tightly together so that Valley wouldn't hear too much of their conversation. Her parents both looked up at Dr. Sumpter and gave him a pleasing smile as he sat down beside them on the waiting room couch.

"May I have a word with you two?" Dr. Sumpter didn't know too much about them— only what the file that was sent over by the state said. Of course, he'd had the two mandatory sessions with the couple during the adoption process and they seemed very well adjusted, but he still hadn't had any real interaction with them to solidify his thoughts concerning their parenting.

"Why yes doctor. Is there something wrong?" Shaundra was a soft spoken woman who did most of the talking for both her and her husband when they brought Valley to his office for her once a week meetings. Dr. Sumpter noticed that even with her pleasant tone, Shaundra's words were definitive and assertive; sometimes coming across as unintentionally cruel. At first glance, it wasn't obvious who controlled the relationship; him being a lawyer with a laid back temperament, and her being a whimsical art teacher at a private elementary school, but after speaking with the pair, it was very plain who made all of the decisions within their household.

"No, there's nothing wrong. Valley just told me that you all will be moving out of town."

"Yes, we'll be moving tomorrow. My husband just made partner at a law firm in Richmond, Virginia. They've been trying to persuade him for years to take the prestigious position, and finally they gave him an offer he couldn't refuse. We are all very excited."

"This is all wonderful news. I think a new environment would be great for Valley. If you need a referral, I know a great psychiatrist who practices there. I'll write their number down for you..."

"There's no need. We feel that Valley doesn't require a doctor any longer. Over this past year, we haven't seen signs of whatever it was you said she has." Shaundra waved the thought of Valley having a mental issue away flippantly with her elegantly adorned hand as she assured the doctor his favor was not necessary.

"Dr. Sumpter, she's such a good little girl, and we're so happy you cured her. We really want her to have a normal life, and quite frankly, she can't do that if she has to see someone like you once a week."

"I wouldn't advise that she stop her sessions. Yes, she seems like she's just fine, but this is a critical time in her treatment, and she needs the structure of these meetings to keep her balanced."

"Well we don't feel that way. We believe that love and affection from friends and family, along with a stable environment will keep her sane."

Dr. Sumpter couldn't force them to make Valley go to therapy, but he could suggest very strongly while he had their ear. "It's true she hasn't had any outbursts in a very long time, and it is a great possibility that she could probably be okay without her sessions. However please reconsider eliminating therapy. It has been proven to really be helpful in maintaining a good state of emotional health."

"We'll think about it, but our minds are pretty made up." Shaundra checked her watch as an indication that she was done explaining her decision.

"It looks as though her hour is up. Jack, be a dear and gather Valley." Shaundra's husband Jack brushed passed the doctor and stuck his head in the door before going in to help his daughter with her things.

"Listen, I can't force you to take her to therapy. Since the adoption has been finalized, you are recognized by the State of Virginia as her parents, and the State believes you know what's best for her. I do wish you all the best, and if you need me, you know how to reach me."

"Thank you Doctor. You have been very helpful and I'm sure she will never forget you."

"As I will never forget her. She's a wonderful little girl. Let me run back into my office and I'll write a prescription for her medication just in case you need it."

"Oh... that won't be necessary. She won't be taking those pills either. Like I said Doctor, she's perfectly fine."

Dr. Sumpter stared at Shaundra in amazement— as if a spider calmly crawled up the side of her face without being noticed. "Mrs. Shaundra, I would not advise you to stop her medication. She's only perfectly fine because she takes those pills."

"I really do believe you're over reacting. Valley hasn't been on them for months now and she's in good health. You didn't even notice any changes in her behavior because she's cured."

"There is no cure for schizophrenia. She's going to always have it, and the only way to keep it under control is with medication. Mrs. Shaundra, the fact of the matter is, your daughter has a borderline personality disorder, and if you and your husband don't know how to handle someone like her, I think it best that you rethink being her parents."

"There is nothing wrong with my child. She's happy, healthy, and normal. She's been that way since the day we met her, and we intend to keep it that way until the day we leave this earth. I truly believe you've made up all of those things wrong with her so that you can continue your warped relationship with a ten year old little girl!"

"I beg your pardon?!"

"Yes, your warped relationship! You've become too attached to my daughter. There's no telling what kind of perverted thoughts you've had about her. Even if we weren't leaving town, we would have stopped bringing her to you, that way, you wouldn't be tempted to touch her inappropriately."

Shaundra ended the conversation with her damaging statement. She then opened the doctor's office door to retrieve her family. "Jack, are you two ready to go?"

"Yes dear. Is everything alright?"

"Oh yes. Dr. Sumpter was just giving me his professional opinion." She smugly turned her head to look at Dr. Sumpter in triumph as he stood in the waiting room baffled at what he was being accused of.

"Bye Dr. Sumpter! I'mma miss ya!" Valley walked past the doctor with both of her parents holding each of her hands. Shaundra rushed them into the elevator and pressed the button to go down and out of the building; never once challenging her sentiments.

Dr. Sumpter went back in his office and shut the door. He'd just been accused of one of the most heinous crimes someone could ever commit. He would never hurt Valley. He loved Valley like one of his own daughters. All of the time he'd spent with her; watching her grow and develop was not only for her benefit, but also for the good of science. He'd made breakthroughs with his way of treating a young child who'd shown symptoms of anti-social behavior in early stages of development that he'd been rewarded for his work... not damned.

The sad truth of the current situation was that he was never going to see his subject anymore, and above of all, he was fearful for her. He knew Valley better than anyone, and he'd seen her before the medication. An overwhelming feeling of dread crowded him as he thought of the potential harm she could bring. He knew it was wrong for her to be off her drug regimen, and if she'd been off it for months, he wasn't sure how long it would take before someone or something triggered one of her "episodes". The whole situation was out of his hands now. If her parents didn't want her on medication or in therapy, there wasn't anything he could do about it. He took one last look at the empty paper cake plate before throwing it away.

Ten years later, and that memory of their last meeting still haunted him. On the day he read the headline about her being arrested for assault with a deadly weapon, he found a way to get in contact with her lawyer in hopes of being some kind of help to her. Once he got approval from Valley's Guardian Ad Litem, Dr. Sumpter took an extended leave from his practice and headed for Richmond, Virginia to help sort out her troubles. When he finally got to see Valley, her mind was so gone from reality that she didn't know who he was. She was literally stuck in the world she'd created in her head. Any and everything she talked about was centered on the young man she'd fixated on prior to being admitted to Central State Hospital in Petersburg, Virginia. Dr. Sumpter shook the old memories of Valley from his focus so he could concentrate on typing the notes into his laptop. Saddened that the little girl that had made tremendous progress so many years ago would never be the same person as an adult, Dr. Sumpter let one tear fall for his patient against his better judgment.

CHAPTER THREE

"Welcome back Valley."

"Thank you Doctor Sumpter."

"Are you ready to begin your session this week?"

"Yes. I think we can begin." Valley folded her hands into her lap and presented Dr. Sumpter with her most agreeable smile. She liked being his patient and looked forward to their sessions. She didn't know why, but she felt there was a bond between her and him that was solidified before she arrived at Central State.

"Where should we start from today Doctor?"

"Well, where would you like to start from?"

"I don't know... We are here In this little room separated by a partition every week." Valley expressed her proclamation meekly.

"I love your visits since you are the only one who comes to see me, but I don't know the purpose of them."

"Well Valley, I'm trying to help you recover some of your memories that may be hidden."

"Oh yeah? What kind?"

"At this point, any will do."

"Oh." There was a pause in their conversation. Valley didn't know what memories he wanted from her. She'd never been interesting to anyone before. She was content blending into the background and enjoying life from the sidelines.

"You mentioned that you don't have visitors. I've also noticed that your family and friends haven't come to see you. How does that make you feel?"

Valley shrugged her shoulders and looked down at her folded hands. "I don't know... I guess they don't know where I am. I would like my parents to come see me though... or maybe my fiancé... or maybe my friend, Giselle."

Dr. Sumpter shifted in his seat slightly excited that Valley had mentioned someone other than Ramses or her parents. The doctor knew Giselle and Valley were close friends through the report she gave the police. In earlier sessions, he'd brought up Giselle, but Valley couldn't remember her.

"Would you like to talk about Giselle?"

"I don't mind talking about her. Heck, if she were here, she wouldn't mind us talking about her either." Valley laughed at her comment thinking about her flamboyant and outgoing friend. "She's my best friend Doc. I miss her so much. We've been through everything together so I don't understand why she hasn't come to visit me. The orderly's let me call her but the number is disconnected. I'm not mad though. She's probably changed it 'cause she broke up with some guy and just forgot to contact me with the new number."

"I see." Dr. Sumpter nodded understandingly which was encouragement for Valley to continue.

"Yeah. As long as I've known Giselle, she's always had a boyfriend. The guys go crazy over her, but she just loves them and leaves them." Valley laughed once again.

"I'm not like her... I wish I were though. She's so beautiful and fun. Back in high school, we use to get in trouble at the drop of a hat over her crazy schemes, but she used to take the blame for everything to keep me out of trouble. She knew how mad my mother would get if she ever found out what I was up to."

Valley thought quietly a little longer about their fun memories before she continued. "You know, she's the one that came up with the idea of going to college at Virginia University. She said we needed to get away from all the snobs at the private school in order to experience real life. I went along with it because I knew Giselle would protect me, and I could be somebody other than the person I was in high school."

By now, Valley was out of her chair and leaning against the partition as she remembered her dear friend. "It's funny... If It hadn't been for her, and that one crazy night, I would have never met my fiancé." She nodded happily in agreement with her outward thought.

"Yup. She introduced me to the man that I love. When Ramses and I get married, I'm going to toast her for setting us up." Valley laughed in excitement of her upcoming nuptials

"You know our marriage day is coming up soon... that's why I have to get out of here Doc. I have to be fitted for my dress, order the cake, and find a church... I've got so much to do..." Valley suddenly went into a fright thinking of all the things she needed to get done before the upcoming wedding. Valley paced the floor, mumbling her list of tasks to complete but only to herself; answering her thoughts with a nod of the head, yes or no.

Dr. Sumpter put his pen and pad down and got closer to the partition trying to check for a crack in her cognitive thinking. "Valley... are you okay?"

Valley abruptly stopped in her tracks and flashed the Doctor an evil look. "What do you think Doc? You're the professional. Aren't you supposed to know how I feel?" The sarcasm of her words oozed from her tongue as she spoke.

Dr. Sumpter uncomfortably cleared his throat. "Valley, I would like to continue my visit with you, but I'm going to need you to have a seat."

Valley made her way to the partition and stood face to face with the doctor. Her expression was filled with anger. Her body shook with rage as she breathed hard against the plastic window that separated them.

"If only you had your knife... If only you had your knife... You could take it and stab it in his eyes for staring at you."

"Yes... and then you could pull it out slowly and then ram it in his throat for asking such silly questions. He's not a doctor. He's a fraud! If only you had your knife, Valley. You'd really show him how you feel."

Valley let her eyes look off and to the left as the voices rattled off ideas on how to get rid of Dr. Sumpter. She smiled with a chuckle as she listened to them talk.

The doctor could see she was not the same person he was speaking to earlier. He backed away from the glass one foot at a time, and sat back in his chair hoping Valley would do the same. But Valley just stood there; chest heaving up and down and her body clinched for attack. The doctor tried to ignore her demeanor by picking up his pen and pad once more, but it was hard to focus with her being in an obvious state of turmoil.

Trying to defuse the moment, Dr. Sumpter made a suggestion. "Valley, we were having such a wonderful conversation about your friend Giselle. Would you like to finish our chat?"

"He doesn't even know we hate her! He's such a horrible doctor!"

Valley shook her head to quiet the voices. She needed Dr. Sumpter to know how she felt about Giselle, and they were now a distraction.

"I don't want to talk about that slut. She's not my friend, and if I ever get my hands on her, I'm going to kill her." Valley was quiet as she simmered in her emotions. Finally, she broke down in a river of tears, and dropped to the floor with her head in her hands.

"What's wrong Valley? Why are you crying?"

"Because! She was sleeping with my man, and she's the reason why he broke up with me!" Valley cried harder as Dr. Sumpter watched. He wanted to sit beside her and comfort her, as if she was his child crying over the breakup of her first love, but he couldn't. Valley was violent and unpredictable. Dr. Sumpter watched her cry a few moments longer uninterrupted before she finally got off the floor and made her way back to her seat. She wiped her tears away with the back of her sleeve and straightened herself up.

"Sorry I couldn't offer you a tissue. They usually have them placed on the table in front of you, but somehow they have forgotten. Next time we meet, I'll tell them to make sure the tissue box is available." Dr. Sumpter looked on with sympathy as Valley got herself together.

"Thank you Doctor, but there's no need. I think I'm cured of this manic thing I'm going through. I just needed a good cry. Mom always said the best medicine for a broken heart is a good cry. I've been holding those tears in for a long time, you know. I'm so glad I finally had my emotional release. Thank you for all your help. You've really been very supportive."

Valley's ramblings about her tears being good therapy weren't believable, but Dr. Sumpter took that as his cue that the session was over. "Well, Valley our time is up. I'll get someone to escort you to your room."

Knowing that her impending release date was not too far away from her thoughts, Dr. Sumpter didn't want to disagree with her about being discharged from Central State.

"Thank you doctor. When I get out, I'll call you so we can do lunch."

As patronizing as he could, Dr. Sumpter retorted, "That would be wonderful Valley. I look forward to it." After gathering his things, he headed towards the door while looking upon Valley who sat in her chair fiddling with her shirt tail. She looked up at him with her mesmerizing green eyes and waved goodbye to Dr. Sumpter while plastering on that agreeable smile once again. Dr. Sumpter waved back at her and left the room. He signaled the orderly that stood outside of Valley's door that the session was over as he headed for the exit.

CHAPTER FOUR

"Oh Valley! I can't believe we are free! We can do whatever we want, whenever we want, and without our parents bothering us!" Giselle twirled around the room landing with her back on her twin sized bunk bed. Valley sat on the bed opposite of her, laughing at how happy her best friend was to start their freshman year at Virginia University.

Being one of the few minorities on campus; Giselle being Latin, and Valley being Caucasian, they were both slightly nervous as they took their first steps onto the urban embodiment of higher education. Virginia University, not being Valley's first choice for the college experience, was Giselle's great idea to apply and accept their admittance. With all of the excitement on the last day of high school, Giselle convinced Valley that they were both tired of seeing the same old people that they'd graduated with. Feeling that they needed the thrill of the challenge, to meet new people, and to enjoy life on the "other side", Giselle pitched her sale of Virginia University, and Valley was sold on starting new in a different kind of environment.

Looking over the vast campus and being a part of the welcoming feeling that older students provided, neither one were worried any longer about adjusting to life at a predominantly African American college.

"A'ight Mami, hurry up with your things. We need to get dressed and go walk around to meet some guys!" Giselle had gotten off the bed and was rummaging through her things trying to find a cute top to showcase her voluptuous body in, along with searching through her makeup bag for the right colors to highlight her exotic features. Valley went through her bags as well looking for something to change into, but only to pass time while Giselle got dressed. Not caring for the frills that came with being a young woman, Valley didn't wear makeup or cute clothes like her friend. She felt there wasn't any need since she couldn't compete for the guy's attention with Giselle around.

Giselle, a real Latin beauty had long light brown hair to graze her tanned skin. When standing beside the embodiment of beauty, Valley saw all of her own short comings. Her physique was tall and skinny with mosquito bites for boobs; unlike her outrageously beautiful friend where guys required a roadmap to direct them around her sexy curves. One of Valley's most distinguishing qualities was her waist length fire red mane. However, Valley's red hair was never styled or garnished with playful bows to accent her features. Instead, it just lay limp and parted down the middle of her head. Her locks had the potential to be full, bouncy, and gorgeous, but it was oily and stringy from the lack of daily maintenance, and it dragged straggly down her back because she never cared that much for it.

Her skin also played a part in her inability to catch the eye of a potential suitor. It was pale and there were brown little freckles everywhere. Her apple green eyes were stunning to look at and most likely her most redeeming quality— if only one could get pass her big long beak-like nose planted in the middle of her oval shaped face. Valley felt her features played against her, making it hard for her internal beauty to show, but she never thought of changing her ugly duckling persona to match how she felt inside herself... only embracing what she thought people saw.

To disguise her awkwardness and the feeling of being less fortunate in the looks department, Valley shadowed Giselle; doing everything her friend did. She tried extremely hard to mimic Giselle's extroverted personality with the hopes that no one noticed how uncomfortable she was in her own skin. Valley followed Giselle around like a lost puppy dog, and would have gone to any school Giselle said to go to, just to have her friend keep her out of obscurity.

Barely finding an outfit she felt would be appropriate, Valley ducked into the bathroom down the hall to change. When she returned, Giselle was already dressed and applying the last bit of her makeup. Giselle smacked her lips together twice to set her lip gloss, and handed Valley her makeup bag. "Here Chica. Put some on."

"Oh no, I can't. I'm fine." Valley pushed the makeup bag away; rejecting her friend's offer.

"Listen Mama. We ain't in Kansas anymore." Giselle smiled cunningly as she continued. "We are big girls now, so we have to look like big girls. Here let me help you." Giselle grabbed Valley by the arm and sat her on the bed beside her.

Valley panicked at the thought of being transformed and not knowing what the outcome would be. "My mom would kill me if she knew I had this on. Besides, I don't know how to wear makeup."

"Don't worry about it! I'll put the makeup on you." Giselle rummaged through her cosmetics to find the right colors for Valley. She began with eye shadow and then some blush. Finally, she applied just a touch of lipstick, and then handed a mirror to Valley. "See how beautiful you are! Aye, you look so different... so sophisticated!"

Valley looked herself over in the mirror and liked what she saw. Inside of herself, she was jumping with excitement at the small makeover her friend did on her, but she played it off by just saying, "Thank you." Finally ready both girls grabbed their pocketbooks, and were out the door.

It was still summer time and the students were all hanging out on the yard with no classes to attend. Giselle loved the excitement and the pulse of the campus. She waved at people she didn't know, and talked to other students while they passed by. If she were walking towards a group of people, she would ease her way up and introduce herself and her friend, Valley. Most people Giselle addressed greeted her warmly. She passed out her number to guys and girls alike, and by the time they got back to their room, their answering machine was filled with invites to parties, student organizations, and study groups. Giselle had successfully started the school year off as the popular chick.

Within the first month of school, Valley noticed that college life with Giselle wasn't what they dreamed it would be. The girls vowed to stay close and not let their different class schedules stop them from hanging out, but it did. Soon after settling in, Giselle found new and interesting people to hang out with before and after classes trying to kill time before curfew.

Valley, on the other hand, found herself shying away from her classmates and holding up in her room playing on the computer, or studying for classes weeks ahead of time. By the end of the first semester, Valley rarely saw Giselle, and there wasn't anyone around to fill her friends place. She was lonely and bored, but she couldn't let on that she was.

"Hey Mama... what are you up to?" Like any other day, Giselle bounced happily into their shared dorm room full of interesting stories from throughout her day.

Valley turned her head away from her books and waved at her friend, surprised that she was back so early. "I thought you had rehearsal's today."

"Oh, I blew them off." Giselle sat down on the bed and took her shoes off. "What are you doing?"

"Nothing really. I was just preparing for next week's assignments." Valley placed her bookmark in the crack of her text book and closed it. She took off her reading glasses, made her way to the bed, sat on it, and then decided it would be best to stretch out.

"Listen... I met some cute guys that I know you'd love. One guy works in the math lab, and the other is a guy from my lit class. The math geek will be perfect for you. He's all into computer science, but the guy in my lit class? Hands off... he has those big muscles that I love." Giselle closed her eyes and wrapped hers arms around herself, as if in a big hug with the hunky well read young man. She opened her eyes again and dropped her hands. "So what do you think? Do you want to hang out with them or what?"

"No, not really. I think I'm going to finish my homework before the nights out. Plus, there's an interesting webisode that's going to come on the computer tonight about the stink beetle. I hear the intricacies of the stink beetle's life can be represented in our own."

Giselle sucked her teeth at the mere thought of being interested in a stinky bug. "Come-on-Valley!" Giselle said with an exasperated tone. "I haven't seen you leave this room since we got here! I never see you with friends, guys, or anything! You're bumming me out!"

Valley became self conscious that Giselle felt sorry for her predicament. "Don't be silly. I have plenty of friends. As a matter of fact, just before you came through the door, I was on the phone with a girl from class. She was telling me about a party next week that we're both thinking about going too."

"I don't believe you Val..." Giselle folded her arms in a huff.

"It's true!" Valley smiled reassuringly. "Plus the reason why you haven't seen me with anyone is because you stay so busy."

Thinking the scenario over, Giselle decided to agree with her friend and congratulate her on becoming independent. "Well, that's great!" Giselle threw her hands in the air as she smiled at the good news. "I was getting a little scared that you were all alone on campus, and I felt bad that I was the one who bought you here."

Valley looked down at the floor. She missed Giselle and wanted her to be around a lot more, but she didn't want to seem needy. Giselle was right. It was officially time for her to make a life on her own, but with all the years of being a shadow, she didn't know how. Valley shook off the feelings of abandonment and focused back on the conversation. "Why would you feel bad for me? I'm having a blast here."

"Liar, Liar! Don't lie to her! Never lie! Tell her how you feel!"

Valley hadn't heard that voice in a long time. She wanted to respond, but she clenched her arm instead. "I've met so many new people here... I'm fine."

"Liar! Liar! Liar!"

"The voices..." Valley thought to herself. As loud as they spoke in her head, she wondered if Giselle heard them as well. Valley pressed her lips together in a tight smile and turned her head to her computer; sneaking a look around to make sure the voices were from inside her head and not from within the room.

"Well, you can catch the end of your drama class. I'm going to finish up on the computer and then head to bed."

"No! Don't do that! It's Thursday! There's a party on campus. Let's get dressed and head over there. I think the Kappa's are throwing it, but who cares. All we want to see is the cute guys!"

"I can't. I have class in the morning, and I have so much to do..." Hearing the voices made her uneasy. She needed some quiet time, without Giselle, to calm her nerves.

"Oh Valley, stop being a wall flower! We're going to this party and you're going to like it!" Giselle's demand to party with her actually took her mind off her worries and drifted her further from the unmistakable voices. Bringing herself back into the moment, Valley watched her pout. Giselle's incessant fretting was uncanny, and Valley couldn't help but laugh at her friend and do as she was told; deciding against needing the quiet time after all. Giselle laughed as well and turned the radio on as they got dressed to go out.

CHAPTER FIVE

"Doctor. Sumpter! Come quick! We need you in room 3121!" The voice on the other end of the phone was frantic. Room 3121 was Valley's room.

"Alright. I'm on my way." He put the phone back on its receiver and grabbed his doctor bag. He rushed out of his office and down the hall. As he approached Valley's door, he could see the orderly's in a struggle with his patient as they tried to restrain her. Valley was a blur of red hair and bare feet. She'd pulled her clothes off, and screamed and thrashed around as she tried her best to pull away from their grasp.

"Get... off... of... me! Keep... your... fucking... hands... off-of-ME!!!"

While Dr. Sumpter was being briefed on the situation, he peeped over the chaos, and into Valley's room. He could see a syringe and a knocked over bottle of pills beside her bed. He looked on her small writing desk and saw a letter written with someone's finger, in what appeared to be red paint. Valley saw Dr. Sumpter looking into her room; making her pause just long enough so that the orderly's could finally get a good hold on her.

"What are you looking at?! You came to stare at me?!"

Before Dr. Sumpter could answer, he felt the warm ball of saliva that Valley hocked out of her throat, slowly slide down the side of his face.

Unaffected by the gross gesture, he wiped his face with the back of his hand. An attendant ran up to Valley and stuck her with a syringe that began to sedate her instantly.

"Can someone please tell me what's going on?" He asked slightly agitated.

"We could hear her screaming from her room, and when we got to her door, we saw her lying naked on her back, yelling, and pulling her hair out."

Dr. Sumpter glanced into Valley's room and saw strands of her red tresses strewn across the bed, all over the floor, and her clothes tossed in the exact same manner.

A resident, who happened to be walking by with their nurse peeked in the room as well, and was very turned on by the sight of naked woman being restrained by so many people. "Yeah, baby... take it all off for Daddy..." He let out a goofy chuckle and grabbed his crotch violently; gripping his groin as hard as he could. "Take it all off for DADDY!" His nurse grabbed him away from the door with extreme force knowing the scene could possibly cause a relapse of his care. "TAKE IT ALL OFF FOR DADDY!!!" The patient spoke angrily and struggled to stay at the door and look at the wild woman but to no avail.

"Come on Harold. There is nothing for you to see here." The muscular male nurse pressed Harold down the hall and back to his room.

"TAKE IT ALL OFF FOR DADDY!!" Harold repeated his sentiments over and over again as loud as he could until his nurse shut him in the resident room behind them.

More people began to come and look and see into room 3121. Dr. Sumpter looked back at the crowd that had gathered in the hall as they watched Valley being prepared to be taken away to the observation ward.

"What was she screaming about? What got her so angry?" Dr. Sumpter now turned to one of the nurses already in the room detaining Valley

"We don't know Doctor." The young female intern spoke up after she'd caught her breath from the ordeal.

"While I was doing my rounds earlier, I peeked into her room and saw her sitting at her desk writing. A few moments later she was banging on the window and screaming about being let out. I should have known something was wrong when I saw her writing... see... she was writing very fast and mumbling to herself. At the time, I didn't think much of it."

"When we heard the screaming and the banging, that's when we came running." The big, balding, white male attendant spoke up; helping to fill in the missing pieces of the story.

"By the time I arrived she was laying on the bed naked just blaring about nothing in particular and pulling her hair out."

Dr. Sumpter went further into the room and picked up the piece of paper Valley had been writing on. The words were repetitive, letters were jumbled together, and the red paint he assumed she penned the message in was in fact her own blood.

i love him he loves me i love him he loves me i love him he loves her she loves him but he doesn't love me because of her so im going to kill that BITCH! IM GOING TO KILL THAT BITCH! IM GOING TO KILL THAT BITCH! BITCH! BITCH! BITCH! BITCH! BITCH! BITCH!!BIT

Dr. Sumpter turned his attention to his doped up patient. He walked over to her. He saw the patches of missing hair and the scratches she'd made on her arm, which is where he assumed she got the blood from to write with.

As the two orderly's held her up, a nurse examined her for any other physical wounds she may have incurred during her tirade. Sedation was coming quickly, but Valley was lucid enough to see the doctor poking around and writing things down.

"You'll be next doc if you keep fucking with me." Valley slurred her words as she spoke. "They say you're next on the list, and I plan to lay down and get me some sleep… and… I need a pillow… and then you're going to get it."

The drug had finally kicked in and the orderly's laid her across the bed as they prepared her for the observation wing.

Keeping a stable demeanor, Dr. Sumpter folded up the piece of paper and stuck it in his pocket to be placed in her medical file later. He walked out of the room and directed his next comments to the supervisor who'd come down to check on the situation. "As you know, Valley is a high risk patient. She is very unstable right now. Since we have no real idea of what set her off, I would like to place her under a seventy-two hour watch.

"I understand Doctor Sumpter. I will have one of my best employees watch over her."

"Please do, and report to me any strange behavior as soon as possible... any time of the day." Dr. Sumpter shook the man's hand and walked back to his office.

The click of Dr. Sumpter's heels echoed through the vacant hall. It was the only sound he heard as the commotion in Valley's room quietly faded in the opposite direction. The echoed noise from his movement was rhythmic and almost melodic. The sound took him back to a memory. A memory of a day he and Valley, almost ten years old, sat in a room alone with only a metronome clicking as it gave her thoughts a rhythm.

"Now Valley, I would like you to relax and listen to the ticking noise. Close your eye lids and feel them getting heavy as your arms go limp, and you feel the weight of your legs as you sit in the nice comfy chair."

The metronome continued to tick, tick, tick as Dr. Sumpter put Valley under hypnosis.

"Valley, try to steady your breathing as you take deep breaths slowly in and out... in through your nose, and then slowly out through your nose. Concentrate on how you fill your lungs with fresh air, and then how you empty out the bad air as your chest collapses."

Valley followed Dr. Sumpter's orders without hesitation. She allowed herself to breathe deeply in and then exhale the bad air out as the metronome continued to tick, tick, tick.

Dr. Sumpter watched Valley breath quietly and slowly until he knew that she was deep in trance. He walked over to her and lifted her hand, to let it flop back down beside her. Dr. Sumpter took a seat beside Valley so that he could continue their session.

"Valley, let's take a walk through a pretty garden. It's a beautiful spring afternoon and we are walking through a garden filled with wonderful smelling flowers." Valley took a deep breath in and out as she smelled the flowers as instructed. Her eyes remained closed as the rest of her body remained still.

"Very good Valley. Now, let's continue our walk and explore our surroundings. To our left, I see a tranquil pond ready for geese to splash around in, and to our right I see a pretty gazebo nice enough to sit and read a book under." Dr. Sumpter put his hand on Valley's arm as he continued. "But look Valley... up ahead. There's a dark wooden shed. I want to get closer to it. Let's take the path up to its door."

Unconsciously, Valley put her hand on Dr Sumpter's hand that has rested on her arm. Valley shakes her head "no". There is a panicked look on her face. Dr. Sumpter takes his other hand and rubs hers soothingly.

"Don't worry Valley. There is nothing to worry about. I'll be with you as we go to the shed."

Valley relaxed her grip as they continue on their way to the shed in her dreams.

"Valley, I think we've come to the front door of the shed. I would like to go in, but I don't have a key. Do you have it?"

Valley nodded her head "yes".

"Can you open the door with the key please?"

Valley nodded her head "yes" once again. Dr. Sumpter watched Valley as she still slept under hypnosis. Suddenly Valley started to tremble as if in fear. Goose bumps began to appear along the back of her arms, and her breathing had picked up to a swift in-and-out pace.

"Valley... what is it? Do you see something in the shed? Remember, I am here to help you. Tell me what you see."

"It's dark in here. I don't see you Doctor Sumpter. Something is in the shed and I can feel it coming towards us."

"Don't be scared Valley. I'm here with you. Nothing can harm you. We are here together. Try to see what is in the shed Valley. Tell me what it is." The doctor's plan was to put Valley under hypnosis to see if he could uncover any memories of the day she was found abandoned. She was just a baby then, but Doctor Sumpter's theory about therapy was that any memory could be recovered no matter how old the patient was when they had the experience. Valley's subsequent rescue from a drainage pipe as a newborn was traumatic enough to leave an imprint he'd hope she'd uncover through intensive therapy.

In past hypnosis sessions, Valley had always come to the shed and has always had the key. This time was different. She'd never opened the door and never had she described the darkness within. For Dr. Sumpter, this was the breakthrough he desperately needed. The excitement of the moment overshadowed the fragile state Valley was in under hypnosis, as she tried to overcome what lurked in the dark wooden shed in her dreams.

"Valley walk into the shed, tell me what you see."

"It's dark in here Doctor Sumpter. I'm scared."

"Don't be Valley. Just walk in and tell me what you see. Do you hear anything?"

Doctor Sumpter watched Valley screw up her face straining to see or hear anything in the dark shed. Finally, her eyebrows went up in surprise. She tilted her head as she tried to hear what noise was coming from the darkness.

"What do you hear Valley?"

"It's a baby. I hear a baby crying."

Dr. Sumpter perked up for he knew it was the early memory he was looking for. "Go to the baby, Valley. Find the baby and help it stop crying. Go to the baby and try to soothe it. The baby is calling for you."

Valley gripped the Doctor's hand tighter. "I can't. There's something in the way. It won't let me in."

"Push through Valley. Walk into the shed and push through whatever it is to get to the crying baby."

Dr. Sumpter watched Valley take a deep breath and hold it in. There was silence, and then Valley let out a shrillful loud scream. Her body started to lurch around as if she were having a seizure.

"Valley! What's happening! Tell me what you see!" Valley said nothing but only continued to scream in terror.

Doctor Sumpter couldn't let her continue the treatment under the stressful conditions. It was obvious that she was trying to escape from whatever was in the shed. He desperately wanted to know what had affected her, but to do that, he'd have to keep her under. However, the ramifications of her dreaming in the nightmarish state could be more than he bargained for.

In a rush, Dr. Sumpter brought Valley back from the garden. Her eyes opened and tears fell fast down her face. She looked around her and saw she was, in fact, in Dr. Sumpter's office. She was safe.

Dr. Sumpter brought Valley a cup of water, and she drank it hastily to relieve her dry mouth. She relaxed back in the chair; almost forgetting what she just experienced.

Doctor Sumpter studied her quietly as she began to relax back into the soft chair.

"Valley, are you okay?"

Valley nodded her head "yes" as she searched the room with her eyes for any remnants of the bad dream.

"Valley, can you tell me what you saw in the shed that got you scared?"

Valley's eyes stopped searching the room. She slowly let them rest upon Doctor Sumpter. Her look was cold. Her breath slowed. She lowered her head so that she looked at him from underneath her furrowed brow. The curl of her mouth was drawn straight as her jaw twitched in agitation. She had the face of evil, and from her look, he knew she'd seen what was in the shed.

"Valley, did you see the crying baby? Did you save it Valley? Did you save the baby from the darkness?"

"No. I killed it."

CHAPTER Six

"Hey Bird Beak! What are you doing over here by yourself? I bet you're picking your nose and eating your stupid boogers!" Portly Jeffery Turnbuckle came up behind Valley while she sat on the grass, near the corner of the school building.

"Hey! I know you heard me, or do you have a bird brain to go along with that big nose of yours?"

"Leave me alone Jeffery Turnbuckle. I'm busy." Valley was preoccupied with nursing the little mouse she found hobbling towards the back of her elementary school, and had no time to bother with Jeffery Turnbuckle and his menacing ways.

Jeffery looked over her shoulder to see what had caught her attention, and saw the mouse Valley was stroking affectionately, along with the toilet paper cast she'd taped on its broken leg.

"That's cool! Give me that!" Jeffery snatched the mouse out of Valley's hand to get a closer look.

"Give it back! It's not yours!" Valley pushed Jeffery on his back while she pleaded for her pet mouse.

"You want it? Well go get!" Jeffery threw the mouse to the edge of the woods behind the school.

"I hate you Jeffery Turnbuckle, and I'm going to tell Mrs. Slate that you killed my mouse!" Valley ran towards the woods to salvage her dead rodent friend, and to give her only companion a proper burial.

"No you won't tell! I'll kick your butt if you do!" Jeffery took off after Valley to convince her telling the teacher wouldn't be in her best interest.

Valley got to the edge of the woods and searched feverishly for her mouse knowing Jeffery Turnbuckle was on her heels. "Stay away from me Jeffery Turnbuckle! You're bad news, and I hate you!"

"You better not tell Mrs. Slate what I did or you're going to get it!" Jeffery pushed Valley and she fell to the ground. Jeffery pounced onto her and began to engulf her in a brutal beating.

Helpless and scared, Valley had to think fast to get Jeffery off of her. She grabbed the nearest stick and swung it square at Jeffery's temple; knocking him out and onto the ground. Right where Jeffery laid half unconscious was her mouse, unharmed and hobbling away from all of the commotion.

"Oh, there you are Mousey! I thought you were dead!" Valley stepped over the injured Jeffery Turnbuckle and picked up her mouse. She looked down at her assailant who was now motionless from the blow.

"He tried to hurt us, Valley. He's gonna come after you when he wakes up."

"Yeah, he's gonna tell Mrs. Slate that you hit him for no reason, and she's gonna believe him and not you!"

"I know you guys! I always get in trouble for what he does. I really hate Jeffery Turnbuckle." Valley scuffed up the dead dry leaves that lay beside Jeffery with her foot, and they all landed in random places on his stomach.

"You know what you should do? You should kill him so he doesn't tell Mrs. Slate what you did!"

"Yeah! That's a great idea! If you kill him, then he can never tell on you!"

"I don't know you guys. This sounds tricky."

"It's not tricky at all!"

"Of course it's not! All you have to do is take that stick and whack him over the head again until you see blood."

"That's all I have to do?" Valley slowly put her mouse in her pocket and picked up the stick she just used to fight Jeffery Turnbuckle off, as she considered the plan the voices thought up.

"Yup... that's all you have to do."

"Then, when the blood comes, drop the stick and walk away."

"Alright... if you say so..." Valley grabbed the stick with both hands and proceeded to swing it down between his eyes. When the stick connected to his face, Valley heard a loud crack and saw the blood ooze from the fracture, just like the voices said it would. His jiggly chubby body twitched from the blow, and then went deathly still as the life left him. Valley carefully inched away from his carcass once she saw the little stream of pee from underneath his body headed her way.

"Good Valley.   Now, put the stick down and go back to the playground."

"Yeah, just get on the swing set and stay on it until it's time to go back to class."

"Okay guys. Thanks for your help. I couldn't have done this without you." Valley tossed the stick to the ground, and ran back to the blacktop. As soon as she got there, the bell rang for the children to line up and go back to class. As Valley got to her desk, Mrs. Slate returned to the class room, and sat in her chair at her desk. She pulled out her attendance book to silently take roll. When she got to Jeffery Turnbuckle's name, she stared suspiciously at his empty seat.

"Class, does anyone know where Jeffery Turnbuckle is?" The class shook their heads "no" except for Valley. Valley sat in her chair with her hands folded neatly on her desk; eyes locked on Mrs. Slate. However, Mrs. Slate didn't notice Valley's demeanor. She was focused on retrieving her missing pupil.

"Thomas, please go back to the playground and check to see if Jeffrey is still there." Thomas rose from his seat and exited the class. Mrs. Slate passed the time waiting on Jeffery and Thomas to return by grading the papers that sat before her.

"Class, please rest your heads while we wait for our classmates to return."

"Yes Mrs. Slate." The 4th grade class recited in unison, and laid their heads on their desk as directed. Moments later, Thomas came back to the class exasperated and terrified.

"Mrs. Slate! Jeffery is dead! I saw him by the woods behind the school!"

The class looked up startled at the news. Valley kept her head rested on her hands just as the teacher instructed.

"Thomas now is not the time for games. Where is Jeffery?"

"I told you Mrs. Slate! He's dead behind the school!"

Mrs. Slate looked at Thomas and could tell something was seriously wrong with Jeffery. "Class, remain in your seats until I return. Thomas, run across the hall and ask Mrs. Prickly to monitor you all until I return."

Thomas ran to Mrs. Prickly's room, and Mrs. Slate went to check out Thomas' story. The class spoke softly amongst themselves about how much of what Thomas said was true about Jeffery Turnbuckle. Valley continued to keep her head on her folded arms sitting quietly.

"Oh dear God! It's horrible!" Mrs. Slate came back to the class with tears streaming down her eyes. "Thomas, come with me to the principal's office!"

Students began to cry while Mrs. Prickly tried to soothe their pain. Valley looked around the class with a blank stare and as cool tempered as can be.

"What are they all crying for?"

"Why are they crying Valley? Is it because he's dead?"

"I don't know why they're crying for him. He was such a mean boy."

"Yeah, Jeffery Turnbuckle was mean and didn't have any friends."

"Jeffery Turnbuckle was mean and didn't have any friends! You are just like Jeffery Turnbuckle... you are mean with no friends!"

"Stop it... don't say that." Valley stated sheepishly and ashamed.

"It's true Valley, you are just like Jeffery Turnbuckle. You should be dead just like him."

"No! That's not true! Stop it!" Valley's voice became more audible; angry with the voices and their chastising comments. Empathetically, Mrs. Prickly saw Valley grieving and headed her way.

Valley shook her head in disapproval to what the voices were saying to her. "Leave me alone! Stop saying those things!"

"It's okay, Valley. Don't cry. It'll all be okay." Mrs. Prickly went to hug Valley, and as she leaned in, Valley yelled out a loud scream and slapped Mrs. Prickly across her cheek without cause.

The class grew silent as they watched the interaction between the teacher and the student. Valley watched them watching her. It made her uneasy and uncomfortable. She pushed herself away from her desk and ran out of the class and into the girl's bathroom. Valley locked herself in a vacant stall and began to cry.

"You said it would be okay! You said it would be okay! You said it would be okay!"

"Calm down little one. Everything is okay. Just stop crying. Now, what do we do when things get bad?"

"Yes, what do we do when things get bad, Valley? Make the pain for all of us go away."

Valley nodded her head with understanding. She reached into her other pocket and pulled out the Swiss army knife she stole from her father's tackle box.

"Valley… do the right thing…"

"Yes, show us the blood just like Jeffrey Turnbuckle did."

Valley put her hand in her other pocket and pulled out Mousey. She watched it sit unknowingly in her hand and then, while its head was turned, she forced the knife into its tiny brown body.

"What a good girl you are!"

"Don't you feel better now? We told you it would be okay."

"Yeah… you did." Valley unceremoniously dropped the mouse into the toilet and then flushed it down. She wiped her tear stained eyes with the back of her hand and took a deep breath. "I feel much better." Mousey's death stung just a little because he was her only friend, but it got her mind off of Jeffery Turnbuckle and his terrible predicament. She grabbed some toilet tissue to wipe her nose and to use on the trickle of blood that was left in the palm of her hand.

"Now go back to class like a good little girl."

Valley walked back down the hall, entered her class, which was now in an uproar with several teachers, the principal, and emotional children all trying to figure out how such an awful thing could happen. With Jeffery Turnbuckle being the least of her worries, Valley strolled back to her desk and folded her arms as politely as before, and waited to begin the afternoon lessons.

CHAPTER SEVEN

"Oh Valley! You will not BELIEVE who I just met! He's a GOD, He's a KING! He's my PRINCE! I can't believe he gave me his number! I could just scream!" Giselle rushed into their dorm room and gave Valley a hug filled with excitement and shrills. Valley had her back facing the door when Giselle entered. Startled but not surprised, Valley disconnected from her mundane daydream to pay attention to Giselle's exciting news. As overjoyed as Giselle sounded, it wasn't unusual for her to come bursting into their room every couple of weeks waving a white piece of torn paper with the number of a new boy toy scribbled on it.

"Let me guess. You're in love." Watching Giselle prance around like a peacock over her new conquest made Valley sometimes wish it was she who could come screaming into their room with news of a new flame.

"Valley, he is so fine! I met him today while I was walking across campus. I was with some of my girls, and when I passed him, he pulled on my arm. We flirted, and then we talked, and now he wants to take me on a date! He's older too, so he has to be a junior or a senior. Ohmygaw, Valley! I think he may be the one!"

"Well, tell me what he looks like!" Valley faked her enthusiasm in doubt that Giselle will keep him longer than the standard two week expiration date for all of her flings.

"He's so beautiful! He's like yellow skinned or something. I can tell he's mixed, but I can't tell with what, but he's bright yellow like the sun." Giselle continued to gush. "He's got these slanted eyes like he just finished smoking a blunt... he made me feel so sexy when he looked at me with those eyes." Her giggles would not cease as she gloated. The torment of it all began to turn Valley's stomach, but she continued to listen intuitively.

"He's not really that tall... like 5'10 or something." Valley shrugged her shoulders as if to say it's not a big deal that he's not as tall as she would like before she continued. "He looks like he's strong with those big hands and muscular arms I saw, and he has a beard and a mustache— but it's shaved really close. Oh! And his hair! He has long wavy hair that he wears in one big ass plat down his back. He smells really good too. I got up real close to him and took a big whiff while he wasn't paying attention." Giselle took in a deep breath; reminiscent of the moment she smelled his manly, but not-so overpowering scent.

Giselle reveled in the moment of his alluring cologne a bit more before she continued. "He's kind of a jokester too. I mean... when we were talking, he was cracking all kinds of jokes and making me laugh. But the best part is... when I was walking away... he touched my booty on the sly."

Valley giggled on queue at the remark; just as she'd done throughout the conversation as her friend recapped her first encounter with the yellow boy with the slanted eyes. "Well, what's his name? Did you give him the fake name like you do all the time?"

"You know she's just rubbing it in. You'll never be as cool, or as pretty, or as fun as her. She knows it, you know it, and we know it. You're a fake! Just like this whole conversation!"

Valley's body ticked and her eye flinched as she shook the malicious thoughts from her head. Now was not the time to show she'd been affected by Giselle's good fortune.

"Not this time. Something about him felt like magic, so I couldn't resist giving him my real name. I think he gave me a fake name though. He calls himself Ramses."

"Ramses? Like the Egyptian pharaoh? What kind of name is that?"

"A name you will never moan in ecstasy! You are not his type! You are a loss, a waste! Someone who will never be fucked!"

"Shut up you! Stay out of my head!" Valley screamed inside her mind to the voices she heard. As self pity became more evident to herself, it was becoming harder for Valley to listen to the dreadful conversation Giselle unintentionally forced her to have.

"I don't know. I asked him the same thing, and he said his uncle picked the name out for him. At this point, his name could be Ricky-Tick-Tavy for all I care. He's going to be mine, and all these little putas walking around on campus are going to be so jealous that I'm dating an upper classman and they gotta settle for these scrawny little boys out of high school."

"Somebody should stick a knife in her throat. Valley... do the world a favor and stick a knife in the whore's throat!"

Valley's body ticked again; blocking the demand she was just given, and continued her conversation.

"Now don't get ahead of yourself. You two just met!"

"Oh, I have no doubt he's going to be mine... just you wait... I'll be calling him my 'Mistah' in no time. And, hey, he's got some friends. I'm sure he could hook you up."

"We'll see. I'm not really trying to date right now." The thought of being popular with the guys was all she dreamed of, but actually being popular with the guys was a whole different ball game that Valley didn't know how to play.

"Ah come on! I've already had my cherry popped and we were supposed to do it at the same time! You gotta hurry up and get yours done!"

"Open up your legs just like your friend and maybe you can be just as popular!"

The voices began again, but she didn't want to listen anymore. She abruptly and inconspicuously pinched her thigh in hopes of focusing on her pain and less on the voices as she continued her conversation.

"Well, I don't want to lose it to some random guy!" Any excuse Valley could think of to prevent Giselle from pursuing her intended actions was the best reply at this point. "I'm waiting for the right one." As Valley lamented over her virginity, she thought maybe losing it to some anonymous hormonal young adult would be better than waiting for 'Mr. Right' since she had no prospects of even a first date.

"Well, I lost mine to some random guy and I could care less. Virginity is so over-rated! Just get it over with already!"

"Calm down Gizzy! I'll do it when the time comes."

"Well, when you do, I can give you some tips on how to take that dang-a-lang!" Giselle began to lean from her waist and Valley got an eye-full of her best friends perfectly round full moon. In shock and with no rebuttal to utter about the tawdry demonstration she would have to endure, Valley covered her face with one hand, but peeked through her fingers to view the performed spectacle Giselle insisted that Valley watch.

"First, you have to bend over and let him take it from behind!" Giselle slapped her ass and then tossed herself suddenly onto the floor lifting and spreading her legs very wide.

"GIZ-Elle! Get off the floor like that!" Valley cupped her mouth in shock, but then burst into the biggest laugh from a mix of amazement and embarrassment.

"Then you have to spread your legs like this so he can get a really good view of your cooch before he sticks his thing-thing in." Giselle began to laugh as she watched Valley double over in laughter and tears.

"Then, once he gets it in, you have to scream and make all kinds of crazy noises like 'uh-uh-uh-uh!' Then he'll nut, and collapse on you like he's all tired and stuff."

"Giz, you are so silly! I can't believe you sometimes." Valley wiped away her happy tears, and helped her friend off of the floor. "When it's time for me to lose my virginity, I promise I won't be coming to you for advice."

"Suit yourself Mama. I've got all the best moves." Giselle blew a kiss at Valley, straightened her hair back into place, and then wiped the dust from the floor off her pants.

"Valley, I'm going to call Ramses and see if he wants to go out tonight since I don't have classes in the morning." Giselle whipped out her cell phone and the white piece of paper with Ramses' number. She barely glanced at the keypad as her thumb rapidly punched the digits into her phone.

"Yo... what up. Who dis?"

"Ramses?" Giselle questionably asked.

"Who dis?"

"Giz from earlier today... we met on The Yard?"

"Oh yeah... sexy mami with the tight jeans! What up Ma?"

"Nuuuthin'. Just wondering what you trying to get into tonight."

"Shit... I hope you. How does that sound?"

"Ummm... that sounds good. What time?"

"I gotta holla at my man an' dem for a minute, but I'll check you out lata."

"Aight, but don't keep me waiting long Ramses. I ain't got time for no games."

"Aight Ma. I got chu. Give me a couple of hours and I'll come scoop you up."

"Aight... lata."

"Lata." Giselle hit the "End" button on her phone to close the conversation.

"Well what did he say?" Valley sat on the bed cross-legged, faking the excitement of her friend's phone call.

"My boo is coming to get me tonight. I knew the moment I walked away he would want to see me again. Come on, let's go grab something to eat. It's going to be a couple of hours before he gets here, and I'm hungry now. How much money do you have on your cafeteria pass?"

"Not much... maybe enough for one more meal. I have to call my mom tonight and tell her to send me some more money."

"Well, I'm all tapped out. I guess I'll have to pull out daddy's credit card and hit the corner store for some groceries. We can grab a slice of pizza while we're shopping." Giselle picked up her pocketbook and keys and headed for the door. Valley did the same; following Giselle's every action. "Let's see if Carl will take us to the store."

"You know he will. He's so in love with you, and you never give him any attention unless you need a ride."

"Hey, don't judge. You're using me to get a ride just like I'm using Carl."

Valley giggled thinking about Giselle's logic. "I guess you're right... slut." Giselle playfully shoved Valley for her comment as they knocked on Carl's door.

CHAPTER Eight

Dr. Sumpter walked up to the hall, and made his way to the door labeled "Electroconvulsive Therapy". Valley is there for her first ECT session. He opened the door to find her laying on the cushioned lab bed talking but speaking to no one in particular. This type of behavior was what bought her to his attention. Her care givers where miffed as to why she directed all of her attention to the voices in her head. Even as going as far as talking to them in hushed tones and only in corners for more privacy. Watching her carry on like that scared them. They'd tried everything to get her to talk to them... her foster parents, but she insisted that it would be best if she only spoke to the voices.

Familiar with her psychological makeup, and knowing firsthand about how the voices consumed her attention, Doctor Sumpter appealed to The Board to start electroconvulsive therapy earlier than the minimum age requirement. Of course this line of treatment... especially for a young girl, was frowned upon and considered a "quack's remedy", but Dr. Sumpter felt Valley had text book symptoms of schizophrenia, which could succumb to the right amount of "shocks" administered to the brain.

Valley heard the click of the door opening and sat up on her elbows to see Dr. Sumpter walk through the door; relieved to see him instead of the unfamiliar faces that'd been questioning her all day.

"Valley, how are you doing today?"

"We're fine Doctor Sumpter."

"Today, we are going to try a new treatment."

"Oh yeah? Is that what that box thing is for?"

"You mean the ECT device?" Doctor Sumpter smiled gently and patted the metal cream colored medical machine, and then turned it on; allowing Valley to hear the low hum it emitted before he continued. "Yes. This little machine will soothe you just enough to quite those pesky voices you keep hearing."

"Huh? The voices? Oh no, Doc. They're my friends. They help me and they talk to me— they keep me from doing bad things. You don't have to get rid of them."

Dr. Sumpter smiled at Valley and rubbed her knee reassuringly. "Valley... do you think everyone has voices in their heads that no one else can here?"

Valley shook her head yes. "Yup. It's called your conscious. Do you have a conscious you listen to Doctor Sumpter?"

The question felt like a double-edged sword slicing him right down the middle. Of course he had a conscious. Other doctors in the facility would somewhat disagree since he treated his young patient as a science experiment instead of a patient— allowing her mental state to teeter on the brink of insanity so that he could finally receive some type of recognition for the kamikaze approach he took towards psychotherapy. Those doctors didn't understand how important his work was, and how much he cared for Valley in other ways. There were issues his young patient had that couldn't be cured conventionally. He had to take drastic measures to save her from herself.

"Yes, Valley. I do have a conscious, but my conscious doesn't talk to me like your voices talk to you. My conscious— and everyone else's works like an instinct does. Instead of a conscious talking to you and telling you to do something or not to do something, it will just make you react or not."

"I don't think so Doc. Your conscious may just be broken."

Doctor Sumpter laughed underneath his breath at the thought of Valley assuming he was the one with the problem. "Trust me Valley, my conscious works just fine. Now lie back so that I may place these two receptacles on the side of your head."

"What do those things do?" Valley pointed to the black metal cylindrical devices connected to the ETC machine.

"These are for stimulating your brain movement. I'll put these on either side of your head," Dr. Sumpter tickled her temples with his finger which made Valley giggle "and when I turn the machine on, they help to stop the voices you've been hearing."

"But Doctor Sumpter," Valley said through her laugh. "I like listening to them talking to me."

Doctor Sumpter nodded his head somewhat understandingly, and then proceeded to turn on the ECT machine. "Here Valley... open wide so I can put this in." Dr. Sumpter held up a pale blue dental tray that could fit the mouth of a child. Electroshocks were known to cause seizures, and the little seizures that a patient has during the session is what soothes the brain; temporarily relieving the patient of anti-social behavior, such as hearing voices. The dental tray kept Valley from swallowing her tongue, or biting it off while the seizures were being induced. He'd almost forgot to order it for her after the board approved his request... too eager to start treatment on his young patient.

"AHHHHH!" Valley opened her mouth up, and let Dr. Sumpter slide the tray in.

"Now lay back and I'll attach you to the machine."

Valley did as she was instructed, and Dr. Sumpter placed the electrode connectors on her temples.

"Valley, I'm about to begin. Once, I start, you'll feel a little tingle but it won't hurt. Just stay relaxed, and this shouldn't take long. After we're done, the tingling will stop and you won't even remember it."

Valley nodded her head, and almost frightened, closed her eyes in preparation.

The ECT machine was warmed up. Dr. Sumpter pressed the black button, and waited for the green light to flash letting him know that the machine was ready to use. While he waited, he remembered the first time she was bought to his attention... a mere toddler struggling to adjust to her foster family. He was told by her caregivers that she'd wake up screaming in the middle of the night from dreams she couldn't speak of. The aggressive behavior she displayed to authoritative figures distressed her foster parents, and the other little ones in their care stayed away from her for fear of being hurt. Her foster family was in desperate need of guidance on how to handle such an unruly child. Dr. Sumpter found her traits fascinating, and perfect for evaluating. He saw a child who showed signs of being a menace to society, but then, he saw a flash of notoriety... and a spark of recognition for "fixing" what he deemed as inherited. He wanted to be the one responsible for changing her, so he took on the challenge of working with the young child, and by any means necessary he was going to prove that his work in early intervention therapy would change the face of psychology.

The green light flashed rapidly, pulling Dr Sumpter back into the moment. "Alright Valley. I'm about to flip the switch." Dr. Sumpter pressed another black button on the ECT machine. The sound of static crackled in the room as the first wave of electricity hit Valley's temples. Her body arched upwards. Her eyes popped open; startled by the energy that was sent through her body. Dr. Sumpter held his finger on the switch of the ECT machine ensuring that Valley received the proper dose.

Finally, after five seconds of electricity surged through her brain, Dr. Sumpter released the button, and then checked the recording of her brainwaves on the ECT device.

"No change." Dr. Sumpter shook his head in disappointment at the reading. "We'll try once again." Dr. Sumpter checked Valley's pupils, wiped the stagnant drool that had collected in the corner of her mouth, and turned the machine on once again. This time, he held the button a little longer than five seconds. He watched Valley's little body tighten from the shock. She was responding properly to the shocks, so he didn't see a cause for concern. He let the button go once again, and checked the ECT reading. "Hmmm... very interesting." Dr. Sumpter smiled at the different activity produced on the reading. "Valley, you are showing progress. Let's try once more." Without hesitation, Dr. Sumpter pushed the black button— holding it just a bit longer than before.

He checked the reading. There was significant change this time around. An ECT session could last up to fifteen minutes, but that time frame was left up to the leading therapist's discretion. Dr. Sumpter looked at his patient to determine if she needed anymore shocks. Her eyes were blank as she laid limp staring at the ceiling. The image almost worried the doctor, as he almost assumed he killed her, but then he saw her chest move up and down to the rhythm of her breath. He smiled to himself, and jotted down some notes on the session before he checked Valley's vitals.

Finished with his notebook, he placed his attention back on Valley. He unhooked her from the ECT machine, and checked her vitals. "All is well." Dr. Sumpter patted Valley's arm; not requiring her to comment on the treatment. Dr. Sumpter readjusted the padded table so that Valley was now sitting up and facing him. "Valley... can you hear me?" Dr. Sumpter turned her head so that she was now facing him. Her eyes were no longer filled with the brightness and wonder of a child. They were dead, and vacant from the electroshocks. "Valley, your treatment is over. Do you still hear the voices, Valley?"

She stared at him as she appeared to think about his question, and then shook her head "no".

"Good. Then treatment was a success. I will have the nurse escort you back to the lobby so that you can meet your foster parents." Valley said nothing. She looked at him, but through him as he continued to talk. Dr. Sumpter walked to the door, and Valley's gaze followed him there. A nurse came in and helped Valley off of the padded table.

"Nurse, please instruct her guardians to call me if she hears the voices again. If we must, we'll administer treatment if the voices come back." Dr. Sumpter turned his attention back at Valley and smiled at her.

"I'll see you again really soon Valley. Now, don't go having conversations with your conscious anymore." Dr. Sumpter chuckled at himself, and then handed her a lollipop; sending her on her way.

CHAPTER NINE

Her orgasm came over her like a title wave. She trembled and moaned with delight as her body welched from the task of letting her hand manipulate her sensitive pink flesh more. She wanted to cum again, but after three climaxes in a row, she knew she wouldn't be able to take another. With the help of Big Black, Valley's new love toy, she was able to experience sensations that her fingers just couldn't manage. After a job well done, and the candles blown out, Big Black was carefully put back in his box. He was a sexy long piece of hard black lacquer coated plastic, shaped like the penis she envisioned her man to have. The sex play between her and Big Black was not for the weak. Valley was still a virgin when she and him hooked up for the first time. Forcing the huge phallic through the barricade known as her hymen was the most intense pain she'd ever had to endure, however, the pain was what thrilled her the most.

On nights when she needed affection, Valley would pull Big Black from his secret place and perform tricks with him steadied between her legs. Never knowing the pleasure of the real touch of a man, Valley used Big Black and her vivid imagination to figure out how the birds and the bees fulfilled their natural desires.

Tonight, Valley was very satisfied with his performance, and after tiring herself out, Valley stuck the box that Big Black rested in back under her bed in the farthest corner up by the headboard. Pulling herself back onto her mattress, she wondered if Ramses liked sex as much as she did. As she fondled the soft petals of her vagina a bit more; making the sensation of sex last longer, her thighs quivered imagining that Ramses touched her just as she touched herself in the silence of her dorm room. Finally done with playtime, Valley removed her hand from her genitalia; more relaxed and engulfed in the "afterglow" Big Black helped produce. Daydreaming out of the small barred window on the wall next to her bed, she thought of the recent date Giselle and Ramses went on that had aroused her so.

Valley found their love affair filled with adventure and passion, and never intended to fall in love with him the way she did. At first, she found it quite absurd that the man she was in love with was sleeping with her best friend, but as the days and weeks passed, and as the stories became more vivid and more explicit, she forgave that one exception and leapt into her new relationship she created in her mind; willing to give it one hundred percent.

It had been a few weeks since that night when Giselle and Ramses officially started dating, and just about every night since they met on The Yard, Giselle would come into the room with juicy details about her date with the man of "their" dreams. In the beginning of Giselle's new love affair, Valley found no real interest in the object of her friend's affection. It wasn't jealousy that kept Valley from caring about her best friend's new boy toy. It was that it was mostly the same "torrid" story every time. However, as Giselle continued to see Ramses, Valley felt there was something about the way Giselle manipulated her storytelling that kept Valley tuned into all of their encounters.

It was one memorable night which danced in her head whenever she made love to Big Black. She remembered how that particular day Giselle had taken her to get a cute skirt to start her new wardrobe off. She tied a knot in a see through fitted white cotton t-shirt that she enhanced by borrowing one of Giselle's beautiful lace padded bras. She put her long red hair up into a high ponytail that bounced around when she walked, and on her feet, she decided she wanted to put on the white Nike sneakers Ramses had recently purchased for Giselle that matched his perfectly.

After getting showered and dressed, Valley went down the steps and hid in the bushes outside of the dormitory to watch Ramses pull up in his sporty black Infinity G35. Students entering and leaving the dorms saw her squatting there, but she nor them acknowledged how awkward the encounter was; she just continued to watch the street for Ramses as if they weren't there. When she saw his car round the corner, she circled behind the building to come back in to it; to meet him as if she just came out.

She walked up to the car, waved a friendly hello at him through the tinted glass window and then heard the door unlock. Giselle eagerly waved back at her, and just like that, they were off into the night to make love underneath the stars. That night forever changed her. She was so completely hooked on their love, that she couldn't help but to participate in their relationship.

It was almost time for Giselle to come back to the dorm room. She looked at the digital clock on her desk which read 8pm, and grabbed her towel and washcloth. She would have been embarrassed if Giselle ever found out that she masturbated while she was away. Unfortunately, before she could reach the door, Giselle came bustling through it with her cell phone attached to her ear and a stack of books in her arms— forcing Valley to step back inside of the room and out of the way.

"Quit playin'! You always say you're not going to come see me, and then you show up on The Yard hollering for me to come down! No

Ramses! Tonight, I'm going to stay home. Maybe that will teach you to stop playing games." Giselle had put her books down and was stretched out over her bed.

"Hol' up Bae... something smells funny in here... I don't know! Hol' up and let me ask." Giselle placed her hand over the phone's receiver as she directed her next question at Valley. "Val, tell me you did not have a freak up in here?!"

"What... a freak? You mean did I have a guy? No... no... why would you say that?"

"Because girl, it stinks in here and you know my nose is sensitive, so I can smell you!" Giselle let out a giggle, and then burst into laughter.

"Ohmygaw, Val! You got your cherry popped!" Giselle bounced on the bed with her knees in excitement for her friend's womanly accomplishment.

"No— I" Valley tried to explain, but Giselle had already made up her own conclusion.

"Ohmygaw, Ramses! I have to call you back! My bestie just had sex and she's about to tell me all about it! I'll call you lata! Muwah!" Giselle hung up the phone and tossed it to the other side of the bed. She sat up and leaned on her knees with a grin that spread across her face.

"Okay, tell me who it was. Who was the lucky man that made you into a sophisticated lady?"

Valley felt uneasy knowing there was a possibility that her secret playtime would become known. She glanced at her bed hoping that

Giselle wouldn't guess that she was in the room alone with Big Black and her imagination.

"You've gotten it all wrong. There was no one here. I don't even smell anything."

"You can't hide it Val. I know you've been up to something. You're all flushed, you've got that silly look on your face, and you've got your towel in your hand. Either you had a guy in here or you were..." Giselle could see how anxious Valley was, and realized that she was in fact in the room by herself.

"Oh... never mind." Giselle folded her lips inward and looked away hoping that she'd save her friend from feeling more embarrassed than she already was.

"I mean... there wasn't anyone up here. You know we can't have boys in our room. I meant to say that I just got back from hooking up with this guy I met a few days ago."

Giselle could see that Valley was trying her best to hide what they both knew, so Giselle just played along. "Oh okay. Well, from the way you look, you must have had a good time." Giselle clumsily scooped up her phone and purse and headed to the door.

"I'm just going to go downstairs and find something to eat. I'm starved. You... ah... go... and take your shower. I'll see you when I get back." Giselle waved one hand and was out the door before Valley could say another word.

"Ah man! She knows! This is so humiliating!" Valley dropped her shower things in the middle of the floor and flung herself onto the bed with tears in her eyes.

Giselle was unaware of Valley's feelings for Ramses— Valley wanted to keep her thoughts private— even from herself, but what she felt for him had become real. Thoughts of Ramses consumed her. He'd become the love of her life, the one thing that got her up in the morning and helped her sleep at night. He was her everything, but it was going to all fall apart now that Giselle knew that Valley had feelings for someone.

Deep in thought and without noticing, Valley had sat herself up on her bed and had rubbed the skin on her arm raw. Out of her panicking trance, she looked down at her pale skin and dug her thumbnail into the reddish part of her raw-rubbed skin. The pain of the fingernail trying to force its way into her body distracted her from the mortification she felt.

"Stop overreacting. You know that she doesn't know about you and Ramses. How could she possibly know? All she knows is that you were having a good time by yourself, and there's no harm in that."

Valley's breathing became steadier as she continued listening to the voices.

"Mommy already told us it was a healthy and natural thing to do it so stop worrying."

"Yeah. Remember that time she watched us rub our privates on the pillow? And remember when we were done rubbing she said it was okay to act out our feelings, and that she even does it sometimes?"

Valley remembered that moment with her mother watching her grind on her bedroom pillow. It was uncomfortable that her mom found her in such an uncompromising situation. She felt the same way when Giselle caught her. The more she thought about that moment and how she was assuringly consoled by her mother's embrace and words about auto manipulation, the less she pressed her nail into her damaged arm.

"Just *take a deep breath like mommy said and then get up and go take a shower. Your secret is still safe.*"

Valley took a deep breath just like the voices ordered and removed her thumb nail out of her forearm. The curved mark her nail left was prominent. Valley massaged it a bit hoping to relax the skin, but she knew the mark was going to be there for a while. With nothing else to consider, Valley gathered her things up once more and headed out the door and down the hall to the showers.

CHAPTER TEN

Giselle noticed that lately, there was something strange about Valley. Over the last couple of weeks Giselle watched her friend move about campus in a way she'd never seen her do before. On days they would meet up for lunch, Valley would sit and chat with her about anything that crossed her mind. Recently, Giselle noticed their relationship had changed. Valley still sat with her for lunch, but she wasn't as chatty as before. Giselle would go on and on about her day, but Valley would only sit; never letting on about anything going on in her life. Thinking about all of the topics that Valley could be secretive about, a smile came over Giselle's face. *Valley had to have found love!* Giselle let out a sigh of relief, packed up her things, and headed back to their room.

Giselle entered the dorm room surprised to find that she had gotten there before Valley. She put her books down on her bed and headed for Valley's to watch the sky out of the barred window as she laid relaxed across her friends bed. As she lay there, she played with strands of her dark curly hair and contemplated what kind of guy her quiet friend would be interested in. She could never picture Valley having a type of guy she really wanted to date because Valley appeared to be such a wall flower to her. She rolled over on her side and let her arm dangle off of Valley's bed. Her fingertips grazed the floor and slightly brushed under Valley's bed. While she swept the floor with her fingertips, Giselle felt something underneath Valley's bed that peeked her curiosity. She reached further underneath and grabbed the hard back book. She sat up cross-legged, and placed the purple leather-bound volume on her lap. On the face of the book was the word "Diary" scribbled elegantly in gold letters. There was a gold clasp lock that sealed its pages from prying eyes. Giselle examined the simplistic security device, and then looked at the sacred golden word once again. Giselle could easily crack the books lock— popping locks was her specialty in grade school, but the thought of betraying a friend's wishes by reading their personal prose made her hesitate for a moment. *"She won't mind if I read a few pages. We're best friends and best friends are supposed to know each other's secrets."* Giselle rationalized to herself. She eagerly pulled one of her hair pins out of her tresses and folded it appropriately to fit into the catch of the purple little book...

7/2010

'John, they've come back. I closed my eyes last night, and just before I shut them tight, I saw them. I don't know what they are or what they want. I don't even know if they saw me watching them. I'll check again tonight just before I shut my eyes tight. If they saw me last night then they won't be back but, if they didn't, I'll see them crawling up the walls once again.'

Giselle was perplexed. She thought to herself, "Who is John? Maybe that's the new guy she's been seeing!" Giselle began flipping through some more of the pages hoping to glimpse a juicy tidbit of her friend's secret life.

8/2010

'John, it's been a while since I've talked to you but I've been busy with my lover. He's so handsome, John. I see him all the time walking around campus, and hanging out with his friends. Once, as I was

walking out of economics, we walked past each other. It was such a magical moment! My hair whipped his shoulder and I smelled his cologne! He smells wonderful! I can't believe my luck! The man that is going to make me his wife is right here on campus!'

Giselle flipped to the next page just as she heard the doorknob jiggle. She hurriedly shut the diary and slid it back under the bed. She laid herself back on Valley's bed and pretended as if she had been staring at the ceiling all along. Valley wouldn't be suspicious of Giselle being on her bed since it was almost routine to find her there catching a breeze from the only window in the room.

"Hey Val. How was class?"

Valley walked into their dorm room and placed her books on her desk. She took her coat and shoes off and then laid on the bed beside her best friend. "Oh... it was class. The teacher showed up late... something about his car, but I could smell the alcohol spewing from his pores. He's such a lush."

"Did you sit that close to know how he smelled?" Giselle scooted over to make room for Valley on the bed.

"Well, yes. I sit on the first row. You know my eye sight is bad." Valley took her glasses off and placed them on the window sill.

"So, you know I'm still curious about that guy you claimed you had in the room."

Valley's body tightened up and her face went flushed. She'd hoped that Giselle would have forgotten about that day.

"What's his name Val? I'm curious. I never see you with anyone... ever! You're either in this room, or roaming campus alone, or in classes! Who is he?! Why are you hiding him from me?"

"I'm not hiding him from you; it's just nothing to talk about. Besides we broke up. I'm not seeing him anymore."

"What do you mean you broke up with him?! I never got to meet him! Agh, Val! You're keeping secrets and we've never done that before! You're making me feel all icky!" Giselle was being over dramatic and pushy. Valley was about to crumble under the pressure of all of Giselle's badgering, but she took a deep breath and said whatever came to mind.

"I'm not keeping secrets from you. I just took your advice and had sex with an available guy. I tried to tell you about him a few times, but you weren't around. I was going to introduce you to him, but we broke up before I had a chance. He was just some lab guy I met, and I won't be seeing him anymore because he's already transferred to another school." As Valley talked, she listened to herself hoping her explanation appeased her nosy friend.

"Val, you actually did it! You had S-E-X!" Giselle gave her friend a big hug, but was slightly suspicious about Valley's explanation.

"So tell me, did it hurt for you like it hurt for me? How long did he last? Was his thing big or was it small? Where did you guys do it? Ohmygaw, did you guys do it in here on this bed?!" Giselle jumped up and started brushing off imaginary koodies from her legs and arms.

"Val, you could have warned me that you had sex on your bed! I don't want to roll around in your juices!"

"Calm down Giz! I didn't have sex in here!" Valley's ears were beat red from embarrassment, so she unhooked her hair from behind them to cover them up. Valley sat up on the bed when Giselle jumped off of it and backed herself into the corner, resting on the wall behind her with her knees drawn to her chest.

"We did it in the science lab after school. We were working on a project after hours and one thing led to another and the next thing I know, I was laid out on the lab table with him humping away. It was no big deal... I barely remember it."

"What! You mean to tell me the biggest moment in your young life was barely memorable?! I can't believe it! I remember every single detail of my first time... where he touched me first, what he smelled like, how my hair was, and even what color and type of panties I wore... a tiffany blue thong with a diamond jewel at the butt crack!"

"Not everyone has a great first time Giz. I'm one of the many thousands that didn't." Valley began to pick at her dirty bitten-over nails out of nervous frustration. She hated being interrogated by Giselle as if she'd committed some horrible act.

"Well, we'll have to change that." Giselle sat back down on the bed assured that she was safe from catching anything remotely resembling koodies. "I have a wild idea... just say yes after you've heard me out, okay?"

"Here you go with your wild ideas." Valley stretched back out on the bed; more at ease now that Giselle had stopped overreacting. "I'll say yes if you promise me I'm not going to end up dead, and that I won't get expelled."

Giselle held up her left hand and put her right hand over her heart. "I promise that you will not get expelled, and I promise you will not end up dead." She stuck her tongue out at Valley after she took her oath which made both girls giggle.

"Okay, yes. Now what is your wild idea?"

"Let's have a threesome!"

"What?" Valley looked at her friend perplexed at such a crazy notion.

"Let's have a threesome! I know the perfect guy. He's sexy, fun, and best of all, he knows how to do it. I bet he'd love to be with you and me together."

"GIS-ELLE! Are you nuts?! We can't have sex with the same guy at the same time!"

"Why not?! People do it all the time! Besides I can guarantee it'll be a good experience, and I can help you with your moves, and you won't have to be nervous because I'll be right there. It's perfect! What do you say!"

"Oh my goodness Giz... my mom will not approve of this! I can't do it. Nope. I won't do it."

"Who's going to tell your mom! This guy has an apartment off campus and it's perfectly safe!"

"I don't even know which guy you're talking about..."

"Yes you do! It's Ramses! You've heard me talk about him a million and one times! He'll be great as your new first!"

Valley's body stiffened once again. The thought of being with Ramses excited her. She'd never been with a guy before and now she had the chance to be with her first love, her first time. Valley rolled back over to face Giselle to see if she was serious.

"Don't look at me like that! Just say you'll do it!"

"Okay... okay, I'll do it!" Valley smiled slyly and gave Giselle a hug. Giselle hugged her back and then got off the bed to grab her phone. She punched in some numbers and held the phone to her ear.

"Hello... yeah, it's me. I got an idea you might be interested in. No... No! Stop guessing and let me tell you. My very best girlfriend in the whole wide world needs to get laid. No! She's not a virgin, but she could use some dick in her life. I was thinking me, you, and her could hook up... yeah I'm serious! No, she's not ugly... she's a white girl with long red hair... yeah, she's down with it. She's sitting right here. So when do you want to hook up? Tonight? Not tonight. We have to get ready... it needs to be special. Let me check with my friend to see if she can."

Giselle covered the phone with her hand while Valley looked on waiting for an update. "Val, can we all hookup up tomorrow? He wanted to do it today, but I wanted us to prepare." Giselle gave Valley a wink and a smile, and Valley nodded her head in eager approval of the next night's plans.

CHAPTER ELEVEN

Valley could hear the steady beep of the machine that was connected to her heart as she slept in the hospital bed. Her head moved slowly to the left and the right as she came out of her sleep. As she tried to raise her hand to smooth out her bed tussled hair, she felt the leather restraints her wrists were bound in. She sighed out loud, and that's when she noticed that she wasn't alone in her hospital room.

"14 days, 6 hours, and 38 minutes." Valley knew the voice, but couldn't quite place from where. She looked towards where the voice was coming from but her vision was blurry. The dark shadow and the feminine voice made her only think of one person.

"14 days, 6 hours, and 39 minutes. Can you hear me, darling? You've been in a coma for 14 days, 6 hours and 39 minutes."

"Mom... is that... you? What are you doing here? What am I doing here?"

"Darling... you've been a bad girl, again." Valley's mother got out of her chair and went to stand by the window. "Honestly, darling. I don't know what to do with you. Your little fits are costing me and your poor dead father a lot of money."

As Valley's mother talked, her vision started to clear up. As she became more alert, Valley couldn't remember the last time she saw her mother. Had it been a year? A few days? She didn't know, but she wished that her mother had chosen another time to come visit her. "Mom... not now. My head hurts. Where am I?"

"Darling... don't be silly. You know where you are. You've been in this wretched facility for over a year now. Had you chosen to go to the all girl's school instead of running away from what your father and I had planned for you, you'd be in your junior year, and interning at your father's law firm. But no, you're here, and practically a prisoner."

"Mom, could you please tell me where I am?"

"Of course dear, we're in the hospital room. Don't you recognize it? Look around you. You've been here several times since that dreadful day."

Valley stared at her mother in a half-dazed stupor as her memory began to unfold. Agonizing grief filled her throat making it hard for her to speak her words. "Mom... it was so horrible how they treated me. He was snatched right out of my arms. What did they do with him? Did they wait for me before they buried him? Did they respect my wishes and wait for me before they buried him?" Tears welled up in Valley's eyes as she felt the emotion of a woman in mourning.

"Here we go with this again." Shaundra huffed a sigh of annoyance before she continued.

"Darling, there wasn't a funeral. I really wish that you would get that through your head so we can get on with our lives!" The rage that boiled inside of Shaundra since her daughter's brink over a mental edge had finally spilled over in the hospital room. She rushed over to Valley and grabbed her harshly by the shoulders, hoping to shake some sense into her only child.

"Valley, it's time you STOPPED playing around and own what you did! I am so TIRED of all of this! Own this mess you created so that we can put it behind us! You don't have to act like this anymore! That woman you attacked has already dropped the charges, so you don't have to keep up this charade! Your father was the best lawyer in the state of Virginia! He has a lot of powerful friends who CAN-MAKE-THIS-ALL-GO-AWAY-IF-YOU'D-JUST-STOP-ALL-OF-THIS!" Valley's mother whispered her last statement hard and harsh in Valley's ear hoping the words would penetrate her daughter's soul, and snap her out of the unnatural condition she resided in.

However, the verbal assault had no effect on Valley. Her mother's presence meant nothing to her. Valley's only concern was the life that was once growing inside of her, but was now gone. The baby was ripped from her without notification. The love that combined within her was now torn from her womb, and all she wanted was to say goodbye to her child in a formal way. Valley turned in her mother's direction, but looked out the window that was opened directly over her mother's shoulder.

"Mama... what happened to my child? What happened to my baby? Did they bury my son with his father?"

"What? What baby?" Valley's mother let Valley go as she looked at her with amazement. With every visit, there was a new turn of events... a new element to the "relationship" she had with the young man that consumed her thoughts. Shaundra had tried so hard to sweep the incident under the rug, but the mess her daughter created was just too big dismiss. At that moment— looking at Valley as a person with a full-fledged mental disorder, she finally came to terms with the fact that her daughter was detached, and would never be the person she wanted her to be. Embarrassment rose up in her, but not for the state that her Valley was in, but for the explanation she'd have to give to all of her friends who knew about what she was going through. Shaundra looked away in shame, and hopelessly gathered her things. She straightened out her tailored suit, and patted her hair back in place before she addressed her daughter one last time.

"Valley... Honey... you were never pregnant, you never had a miscarriage, and you will probably never be a mother. That young man you speak of never knew you. Living in this hospital is your reality from now on. You will never leave here because there is something terribly wrong with you. I hope for your sake that you pull yourself together. I've done all that I can for you, and will do nothing more." Valley continued to stare at her mother trying to absorb what she heard.

"Don't say that mom. I was pregnant with your grandchild. My son was beautiful and conceived in a moment of passion." Shaundra's words were lost on her. Valley couldn't comprehend that her mother had resounded her final farewell. She instead looked off in the distance as she went back in thought to the night she and Ramses shared a passionate moment in his car.

"That baby was truly a love child." A tear glistened in the corner of her eye as she thought about her child fondly.

In disbelief, Shaundra shook her head at how her daughter overlooked her last plea (as heartless and stiff as it was) to come back to reality. She took one last deep breath; exhausted and out of hope, and walked to the hospital room door. "You have embarrassed your father and me with who you've become. This will be the last time we see each other. May God have mercy on you for what you have done to all of us."

Shaundra put her hand on the door handle to pull it open, but then hesitated. She walked back over to her daughter who now looked lost in the hospital bed, grabbed her pale hand and stroked her red hair. She gently tilted Valley's chin upwards, so that they looked at each other one more time.

Coming out of her daze, she saw her mother's beautiful almond shaped eyes looking down upon her; Valley felt the connection and the loving warmth of a mother's security. "Mommy... you are the best mommy ever." Valley spoke as a child, and Shaundra sensed that her grown daughter was now her baby once again.

Valley looked at her in wonder... perplexed at the sorrow her mother displayed. "Mommy, you look sad. I'm going to draw you a picture of butterflies and unicorns. Will that make you feel better?" Shaundra touched her finger tips to her own lips and then to her daughter's cheek. Valley smiled at the gesture. "Mommy do I belong to you? Do I belong to you and daddy?"

"No darling. Not anymore." Shaundra let go of Valley's hand and turned harshly towards the door. Valley's mother dared not look back for the sake of relenting on her final decision to leave her daughter's side. She grabbed the door handle once more, and whisked it open.

"Mommy...."

Shaundra paused, but did not turn to look when her daughter called out for her. As dignified as she could, she pulled her shoulders back, patted her hair close to her left temple, and closed the door behind her.

"Mommy..."

The door made a loud echoing click behind her making Shaundra blink hard. A slight tremor came over her as she fought back tears that started to become noticeable. *"I love you Valley, but not like this."* Shaundra thought to herself as she picked up her pace; catching the elevator going down to the main level. *"Not like this Valley."*

She punched the lobby button on the elevator panel, and as she felt the elevator going down towards the outside world, she tried hard to put Valley and her problems in the back of her mind. Her elegant diamond watch showed it was thirty minutes before she would meet her friends for lunch, and she didn't need her last farewell to spoil it.

CHAPTER TWELVE

Valley was on pins and needles about her date with Giselle and Ramses. As she sat in the shared dorm room, on her twin bunk bed, waiting on her friend to finish primping herself in anticipation, Valley imagined how the night would end— hopefully wrapped tight in Ramses arms, right after solidifying their love for each other with orgasmic spiritual intercourse. The thought of her and Ramses' first real encounter thrilled her, and brought up so many life altering questions all at once: Could she be as fabulous as Giselle was known to be in the bed, with the man they both shared intimate thoughts about? Would her personality shine through so much, as they shared a laugh over dinner that he'd come to the realization he really wanted to be with a sweet and timid soul such as herself? How great would it be that he'd see her as a far better prize than her overtly sexual, pinup style physiqued friend.

"Valley! You ready for our hot date!" Giselle twirled away from her reflection in the wall length mirror they shared. Giselle looked gorgeous in her fitted black dress with the cut-outs strategically placed from chest to navel, but her gleeful twirling stopped once she laid eyes on Valley's drabtastic outfit. "Umm... so, are you going to get dressed? Ramses and his friend will be here any minute."

Valley's fantasy about her being swept off her feet by Ramses came to a halt when she heard there would be an extra man involved in her threesome. "What friend? You never said anything about a friend coming with him."

"Okay... so, don't be mad." Giselle pleaded. "Ramses called me back with a better idea, and I just went along with it."

Valley became slightly irritated that plans had changed without her being notified. There was only one guy for her, and she was not going to soil her body with another man's dingy white cum. She'd been saving herself for the right man, and Ramses was it. Giselle was absolutely not going to spoil that for her. "Well, I'm not going Giz." Valley folded her arms together in resistance. "You said a threesome and now it's a couple's thing. I don't know this guy." Valley laid back on the bed in preparation for the fallout from her friend.

"Ay dios mios, Valley! What are you putting me through! Don't do this to me Val! You said you would do this as long as I didn't get you killed or expelled! You're about to *EMBARRASS* me if you don't go through with this!"

Valley considered her situation as she continued her protest. Sure, Giselle had tricked her, but if she stayed in the room tonight, she would miss her chance at making real love, with a real man. After thinking it through, she pulled herself from the bed, smoothed out her ill fitted t-shirt and faded denim jeans, and stood up. Slipping her Family Dollar flip flops over her unpedicured feet and chipped toes, Valley smiled at Giselle and said, "Okay, you win. I'm ready to go."

Giselle looked at Valley in desperation and shock. "Valley what do you have on?! Don't tell me you're going like that!"

"What... should I change my shoes?"

No longer worried if Valley would participate or not, she was more concerned with making Valley over before the guys showed up. "You need to do a lot more than change your shoes! Could you look a little more less appealing?! We're not trying to make the guys work that hard for the punani!"

Frustrated at all the sudden demands, Valley couldn't understand what all the fuss was about. She thought she looked appropriate for a night of just sex, but plans had changed, and whatever they intended on doing tonight must be a big deal, so she had to oblige since she agreed to the evening. "Should I take my hair out of this ponytail?" Valley slid her ponytail holder down her stringy red trestles; leaving her hair to hang limp down her back once again.

"Amongst other things. Here, step over to my side of the room. You're a little smaller than me, but I think I have something you can fill out. Good thing we wear the same size shoes 'cause I'd be forced to stuff your piggy's into my stilettos." Giselle rummaged through her closest and through her drawers until she found a leather-like cheetah print dress that fit Valley just right.

"And here. Put these red pumps on while I do your makeup..." Giselle went to work on Valley's face; meticulously adding blush, lining her eyes, and curling her lashes. As Giselle placed the last bobby pin into Valley's tosseled hair, the cell phone rang flashing Ramses' number.

"Hey Boo! Yeah... we ready. We'll be down in two." Giselle hung up the phone, and turned Valley towards the mirror revealing her new look.

Valley was in shock. She'd never seen herself look the way Giselle made her look.

"Well, what do you think? You like?"

Valley smiled at the vision of beauty that undoubtedly was her own reflection. She even struck a hint of a seductive pose; seeing a small inclination of sexuality she never could have envisioned. Before she could admire her grace any longer, Valley felt the sudden pull on her arm as she was being dragged out the door.

"Come on! They're waiting for us!" Before they exited the room, Giselle paused, turned to Valley, and gave her a kiss on the cheek. "Thank you for doing this, Mami."

Valley smiled with appreciation and was officially ready for her date.

CHAPTER THIRTEEN

Four hours into the evening, and the night felt more like an excursion through Richmond, than a date. Dinner at T.G.I. Friday's, bar hopping downtown in "The Bottom", and then cuddling at Skyline Drive was just exhausting. However, just being mere inches away from her one and only made all of it magical, even though she was sharing their moment with two others. Leaning on the metal bar that separated her from the edge of the cliff they stood on, Valley looked up at the stars thinking how nothing could top what she felt for him... not even the hoochie or the third wheel.

Valley looked over at Ramses. Giselle's head quaintly leaned on his shoulder as he puffed on the blunt he rolled in the car before they got out to enjoy the view. She sucked her teeth and thought that *should be me with him and not her.* She looked away disgusted that everything about their night was perfect except for her being stuck with Ramses friend, Chad.

"You alright? Are you cold?" Chad saw that Valley had turned from enjoying the moment to looking annoyed. He took his jacket off and draped it around her shoulders hoping that would make her comfortable. Valley wasn't accepting of his kind act and shrugged the jacket off of her, where it landed in the gravel.

"No thank you". Valley inched away from Chad as the voices began feeding her negative thoughts.

"Why did he come? He's ruining everything. If only we could accidentally tip him over the rail..."

"Yes accidentally... but then, we wouldn't have our moment with Ramses. Do not think of hurting him Valley. Chad is our way to Ramses."

"Don't put this on me! You're the ones who like to hurt people! Now shush before someone hears you." Valley had tucked her face into the side of her neck hoping nobody noticed she was in a private conversation.

Chad picked up his jacket and brushed it off. "Sorry. I thought you might have been chilly sitting out here."

"I'm fine. I'm just ready to go." Valley glanced over at the two lovebirds once again. *Giselle, I hate you so much right now.* Valley gritted her teeth as she coveted the prize position of being by Ramses side.

"You're ready to go?" Chad perked up as he misinterpreted Valley's body language, and looked over at Ramses to get his attention. "Ramses, I think it's time to leave. Valley's ready to go." Chad winked at Ramses, and Ramses returned the wink with a nod and a smile.

"Ladies, I think it's time to really get this party started."

Giselle began to laugh and then turned to Valley. "Girl... you are about to get it!" Ramses kissed Giselle on the cheek, scooped her up and carried her to the car.

Valley looked at Chad in astonishment as she wondered what they were planning. Chad returned the smile, bowed, and extended his hand to the car.

My lady, right this way. Your chariot to desire awaits."

Skeptical and with no other options, Valley walked back to the car, not knowing what to expect.

On the way to their destination felt like a secret joke Valley wasn't allowed to know about. There were whispers and giggles as Chad, Giselle, and Ramses assured Valley over and over again to trust them, and that she was going to thank them later.

"Here, put this blindfold on." Giselle had reached into her pocketbook and pulled out a purple satin scarf and handed it to Valley.

"What for?" Valley looked out the window and saw that Ramses had turned down a dark dirt road.

"Valley, you said you trust me, so just put it on. I want you to be surprised when we get there."

"I thought we were going back to Ramses place. We are nowhere near campus."

Chad placed his hand on Valley's knee and rubbed it slowly. "Valley, don't worry about it. I'm going to take really good care of you. Please put the blindfold on. You'll ruin the surprise if you don't."

"But I don't want to put it on. I'm not comfortable with any of this."

Ramses slowed the car down to a crawl then a halt. He put the car in park, and turned himself to Valley in the backseat. Valley looked into his mesmerizing light brown sparkling eyes. She watched one side of his mouth turn up to make a slanted smile. He took his hand off of the wheel and touched her slightly on the arm before he began to speak.

"Baby girl. I've planned a really nice night just for you to enjoy. I put a lot of effort and hard work into making this a night you will remember. Could you please let Chad place this purple blindfold on you so that we can get the night started? You look so beautiful tonight, and I can't wait to see what your body can do. Please put the blindfold on for me." Ramses ended his plea by kissing the top of her hand with his soft puckered lips.

Valley's panties were now moist. His words were low, and as they rumbled through her ears, the vowels and consonants that floated in his tone stimulated every point of pleasure on her waifish body. She had no words for the answer she wanted to give him, so she took the blindfold from Giselle and handed it to Chad.

"Thank you sweetheart. I promise, you won't regret this."

After putting on the blindfold, the whole night was shrouded in darkness. Once the car was parked, she held a strong hand whom she wanted to assume was Ramses as she was escorted from the car, up stone stairs, into an elevator, and into a place that smelled of heavy incense, and filled with other people touching her, welcoming her, and making suggestive promises in her ear as she walked pass them.

"Valley. You are safe. I'm with you". Giselle whispered into her ear. "By the end of the night, you'll be an official member of our little freak squad." Giselle giggled and gave her a kiss on the cheek. The manly hand that held hers let go, and Valley heard a door lock behind her.

The room stayed pitch black as the blindfold came off. She saw no one, but she heard deep inhalations, and quite moans all around her. She was scared to move. She stood still and waited for someone to tell her what to do.

"Valley... finally you will become a woman!"

"Yes! We will blossom and become a full woman tonight."

"I'm scared..." Valley whispered aloud thinking only the voices heard her.

"Don't be." His voice was deep, but she didn't know who it belonged to. The man with the strong voice scooped her up into his arms and made her straddle him as he carried her to another part of the room. He then laid her down on a soft cushiony place. More hands began to grab at her.

"It's so dark in here..."

"Don't worry. I'll help you find your way around."

"Who are you?"

"The man of your dreams."

"Valley! It's him! It's Ramses! He's chosen you!"

"Yes! He's chosen you! You were right! He wanted you more!"

In the darkness of the room, the smile that took over her face was invisible. There was nothing more pleasurable in knowing that the man she wanted, wanted her more. Valley relaxed into her soft spot on the floor and let thoughts of Ramses take control of her body.

She felt him faintly kiss her décolletage. It sent chills up her spine. She'd never been kissed like that before. With his teeth, he nibbled at her breast that wanted so desperately to be released. Valley obliged and unhooked the dress while he made his way back up to her neck.

"He makes me feel so good you guys! He's even better than Big Black!"

Her dress was undone, and she'd taken off her shoes while he stayed preoccupied with finding a way into her panties. Spreading her legs ever so slightly and without any objection from her, he took that as the "go ahead" to proceed without caution.

His body laid on top of hers, his penis as his guide. He slid it smoothly into her opening; only applying a gentle thrust to help himself settle into her warm soft pillowy goodness.

"Valley... he's entered us... what do we do now?"

"I don't know what to do..." She whispered into his ear.

"Stay calm and I'll take care of it." He planted a kiss on her lips and began to go to work.

Valley's body heat rose as she paid attention to the rhythm his body created between them. He pumped his pelvis front to back as his penis went in and out of her. His shaft was rock solid and worked effortlessly to please her. She moaned along to his movement. Nothing had ever felt like what she was experiencing in that dark room with all those unfamiliar people around her. Her sounds of ecstasy mingled with others. The symphony of sex excited her, and she found that her voice increased in volume as she felt her river begin to flow.

He picked up his pace, but didn't take it to full speed. He lifted one of her legs over his shoulder and pounded into Valley a little harder than before. Her vaginal walls were pliable after she'd cum the first time, and he was now able to slip and slide deeper inside.

The excitement of the moment had Valley lost in her own world. She didn't need to close her eyes and imagine Ramses making love to her as they floated away on a cloud. In that instant, she was on her cloud, with her man, enjoying a sacred moment.

"I love you, Ramses." Valley moaned her proclamation as she climaxed once again. She didn't wait for a response from her lover, but her sentiments sent him into a frenzy as he pumped her harder and then faster.

He flipped her over and grabbed her thighs, aligning her pelvis with his. Her legs were wrapped around his waist and her feet locked behind his back, as she lifted herself onto the palms of her hands with her arms locked straight. Valley didn't know what to do, but before she could ask, his dick drilled in and out of her pussy. He rammed her like he was pushing his way through a door, and the sound of their skin slapping was all she could hear. There wasn't any pleasure in that position, but she endured for the sake of her man; knowing the sacrifice would be appreciated in the end.

"Here I cum baby... I'm about to bust!" He held her hips tight as he came. His white creamy juice spilled out of her; dribbling down the back of her thigh. She wanted to wipe it up and lick his specimen, but had she moved from her position, she would have fallen on her face.

"Ready for round two?" He huffed and puffed as he shifted her onto her knees. "It's time for doggy style."

"It's time for what?" She asked, as he entered her from behind, and placed his hands on her hips for stability, and began to pump vigorously once more.

He grunted and moaned as he enjoyed the straight shot down her wet canal. Valley enjoyed the wave of sensations her body experienced as his warm meat slid in and out of her, but she was distracted by the thought of not performing the anticipated move correctly.

"Valley, you're doing it all wrong! You can be so incompetent when it comes to making love."

"It will be all your fault if he doesn't love us."

"Sshh... I'm concentrating! I have to do doggy style right to make him love me!"

As his body pushed into hers, Valley's instincts kicked in, and she began to pant heavily.

"Yes, Valley! That's it!"

"You are absolutely correct! Panting is just what dogs do!"

Valley then let out a low growl as she felt his piece stiffen for his climax.

"Bark like a dog for him Valley, he'll be able to cum better if you bark louder!"

"Grrrrruff! Grrrrrruff!" Valley let out a bark confident it was the right thing to do.

"Very good Valley! Doggy style is easy!"

The voices continued to coach Valley as she barked louder, and louder. Couples, who were making love around her, giggled not knowing what kind of fetish play the unknown female was in to.

"Chill ma... you're blowing my nut..."

"I'm sorry Ramses... I thought I was supposed to bark to—"

He covered her mouth to shut her up. As he began to pump faster and faster, he forced himself in deeper until he quickly pulled out and came all over Valley's back. He let out a long moan in satisfactory completion as he shook the rest of his load onto her butt checks.

"You did it Valley! You did doggy style for the first time and it was perfect!"

Valley turned over to lay with her partner in sexual bliss, but the lights came on exposing everyone in the room.

"Alright you sexy people, it's time to switch partners. It's a lot of new-comers here, so pick someone you don't know to hook up with. Lights will be back off in two minutes, so make your choice soon."

As the announcer spoke to the crowd, she turned to smile at Ramses who'd been holding her the whole time, but she was astonished when she realized it wasn't him she'd been with.

Valley pulled away from the stranger she'd been stuck with since she walked through the door. "You're not Ramses." She said in an offended tone.

"Who? Naw, boo. I'm Toney." He wiped the sweat from his brow, while he layed out in exhaustion. "Lay it back down girl. I want another round with you. And hey… what was all that barking and growling about?"

Valley didn't stay to answer his question. She scooped up her clothes and angrily made her way to the door.

Giselle saw Valley leaving and sensed she was having a bad time. "Val! Where are you going? Is everything okay? Did that guy hurt you?"

Valley turned to her friend feeling betrayed and ready to give her a piece of her mind.

"Val, don't leave… I thought you would like this."

"It's not what I expected Giz. You said you wouldn't leave me, and when they turned on the lights you weren't there."

"I'm sorry Valley. You are in a safe environment, so I knew you would be taken care of. Here, come with me. Ramses and I are over there on the bed by the window. Why don't you come chill with us, and Ramses can be your next partner."

Valley thought on the idea for a moment and reluctantly agreed to it. "I'll do it, but if you leave me again with a stranger, I'm out of here."

"I promise not to leave you again." Giselle smiled, gave Valley a reassuring hug, and then led her back to the bed.

"Lights out in 5... 4.... 3... 2... 1!" The announcer flipped the switch on the lights and the room was dark once more.

It was the next morning. Outside of the window overhead, the faint sound of birds could be heard; signaling the start of a new day. Rolling over in the unfamiliar bed, and having her arm flop over a hairy but muscular chest made Valley feel like a true woman. Her smiling morning yarn assured her that the double date was well worth it. Not only did she have her very first real encounter with the man of her dreams, but she was able to wake up next to him with the heat of his morning breath on her neck. She lingered in the closeness of the moment imagining what it would really be like when they finally shared their bed together. She snuggled into the curve of his fetal position to get a better listen of his rhythmic heartbeat, but the bustle of her movement made him abruptly roll over; making them now back-to-back. Valley's blissful moment of morning love was now over.

It was early Sunday morning. In a couple of hours it would be time to meet her study group. She fluttered her eyes all the way opened, stretched and sat up in the bed. She looked at herself in a nearby mirror, and saw the history of the night before in her tangled hair and smeared make-up. "Giz..." Valley tapped her friend who slept peacefully across the foot of the bed.

"Giz... wake up. We have to go."

"Ummm.... Valley. Not yet." Giselle woke up just enough to crawl to the top of the bed and get underneath the covers.

"Giz… yes. I have to go. I have a study group to prepare for." Valley rocked her friend's body with her hand, but it didn't help. Giselle was back to sleep in no time. Valley let out a heavy sigh and scooted herself out of the bed. She stooped down and gathered her clothes from the night before off of the floor. As she stood back up, she planted a soft goodbye kiss on Ramses' face without anyone else looking. Valley put on her clothes as quietly and as quickly as she could so as to not stir the others in the room. Making her way to the closed bedroom door, she stepped over a few sleeping bodies that were snuggled beside each other for warmth or intimacy. Valley cracked the door just enough to slip through it hoping not to disturb the others with the morning's light, but she found her attempt was unsuccessful.

"Valley… is that you?"

Valley heard her name whispered in a raspy voice from inside the room and from floor level. Valley looked in the direction of the voice hoping it was Ramses realizing his beloved had left his embrace.

"Valley, are you leaving?"

Valley strained to see who hurriedly tiptoed towards her without the grace and consideration she'd displayed moments before. The figure she fought to see in the dark room and without her prescribed glasses finally became recognizable. Once she got a good look at the manly figure approaching her, Valley rolled her eyes to herself as she continued out the door.

"Wait for me Valley. I want to talk to you."

"What do you want, Chad?" By the smile on his face, he hadn't caught the tone of her voice informing him that she was not interested.

"I didn't know you were leaving so early. Can I ride with you back to your dorm?"

"No. I don't think that would be a good idea. I have a study group in a couple of hours that I have to prepare for. I'll talk to you later." As Valley began to walk away, Chad picked up his pace continuing his conversation with her.

"Oh, well, I was hoping to see you again. I had a really good time with you last night." As adorable as he looked standing as tall as 6'7" with spiky blonde hair and his surfer boy looks, Valley's eyes were only checking for one man, and Chad was not him.

"It was just dinner and sex... no big deal."

"I was hoping to get to know you better. You seem like a girl with her head on straight. Plus, we can always double date again with Giselle and Ramses, we— "

"Look Chad. This thing we did last night— this orgy I was unaware I was going to be a part of is not my scene. I'm not like this. So if you could please excuse my absence from any other planned events with you and your friends that would be great." Valley reached the elevator in the massive home she finally realized she'd been brought to the night before, and hit the down arrow."

"Correct me if I'm wrong, but no one twisted your arm to join the party. I was told you needed a little excitement since you'd been studying since the day you got to campus."

"Look... I know what this was. You don't have to pretend to be interested in me anymore. You did what you were asked to do and now your job is done." Valley pushed the elevator button repeatedly even though she knew it wouldn't make it come faster.

"What are you talking about? What job?"

"Don't play dumb."

"Honestly, you got it all wrong. Ramses told me his Shawty had someone they wanted me to meet. I went out with you on the strength that you was chill. If you ain't tryna kick it, or if you telling me I was your jump-off then it's cool. I'll just back down, but I was trying to get to know you if you don't mind."

The elevator chimed and its doors slowly slid open. Valley stepped between them, and then turned to face Chad. "Thanks, but no thanks. You aren't my type. Besides, I already have a man." The doors to the elevator closed, and Valley was on her way back to the front door, hoping to catch a ride with anyone leaving. Chad was left staring at Valley, with a silly look of confusion on his face.

CHAPTER FOURTEEN

"Doctor Sumpter, can I ask you a question?" Valley laid on the cold laminate floor with her cheek pressed firmly to it. The chill the floor emanated had a calming effect on her, which she felt she desperately needed. Lately, for no real reason, her body felt wild on the inside. The effects of the uncontrollable feeling were horrific. She wasn't sleeping very well and she was barely eating. It also didn't help that they wouldn't let her out of her sterilized room long enough to enjoy fresh air, or to sit under an inviting tree.

"Yes Valley. What would you like to ask?" From his lethargic demeanor, Valley noticed today that Dr. Sumpter wasn't his pleasant self. Usually the doctor would greet Valley with a hearty hello when he entered the counseling room from the other side of the glass. He'd then set his chair up so that he could be close to the window pane divider.

There wasn't any doubt that the relationship between Dr. Sumpter and his patient, Valley was tumultuous at best, but he had the uncanny ability to know when Valley was having a better day than most, and he played on that to get more information about her mental state, since she was more than willing to talk when she was in a good mood. Today, however, the doctor didn't seem to care. He appeared to be less interested in Valley, and channeled that feeling into his silence. Valley picked up on his distant demeanor and decided she was going to be the doctor for their session. She quickly got off of the floor and sat erect in her chair. Valley crossed one leg over the other and folded her hands into her lap. She "pursed" her lips together in a dignified way and began her therapy session.

"Now Doctor Sumpter, why don't you tell me what is on your mind. Explain to me, as best you can, how fucked up you are." Valley laughed at her words; finding it very entertaining for someone else to be in the "hot seat" for a change.

The truth was, Dr. Sumpter didn't know how to feel at the moment, and even though Valley's words meant only malice, he felt that he was actually a fuck up in regards to thinking he would be able to help her. He'd tried to ignore suggestions from his colleagues that she may have been beyond professional help, but it hit him before his session with Valley began, that he'd been trying for months to break through her mental block, and his efforts to bring her back from her crazed and mixed world were a lost cause. He'd failed as a doctor, and all of his hard work proved that intervention therapy hadn't worked on Valley. Dr. Sumpter stared at his patient— her not knowing him, and him seeing a failed experiment.

"Dr. Sumpter, did you hear my question... are you listening to me Dr. Sumpter?"

Dr. Sumpter was tired of playing games with her. He took a deep tired sigh, got up from his chair and left the session early. *"This is pointless..."* he defeatedly thought to himself.

Valley watched as the doctor listlessly left the room. When the door behind him shut, she cracked a half smile and began to giggle a high pitched hysterical sound between her tightly closed lips. Dr. Sumpter could hear the eerie sound through her closed door knowing it would haunt him for the rest of the evening.

"Excuse me nurse..." Dr. Sumpter tapped the orderly on the shoulder to catch the young lady's attention. He spoke louder than usual to drown out Valley, who'd moved closer to the window on her door to continue her taunt. She banged on the pane of it as she continued to laugh at him as if mocking his failings. It was annoying to hear and watch her, and he quickly wanted to get away. He hastily spat out, "Could you please escort my patient, Valley back to her quarters? I'm done with her for today." The nurse nodded her head in slight acknowledgement of his instructions as he bustled down the hall and back to his office.

"Come on here Valley. Don't cause no problems while you with me. I'm trying to leave in thirty minutes, and don't have time for you to be acting up right as my shift is ending. I heard what you did the other day... taking your clothes off, falling out and whatnot."

Valley shifted her focus on who'd entered the room, and realized it was her favorite nurse standing there. Valley smiled genuinely at Nurse Barnes who greeted her with the same welcoming smile. "Hey Roxanne! You know I'm not going to cause no problems when I'm around you. I only give the other nurses a run for their money 'cause I don't like them." Valley gave Nurse Barnes a hug before she exited the confined therapy room.

"Good 'cause I have a hot date tonight with my man that I don't want to be late for. You be good for the rest of the evening, and I'll tell you all about it tomorrow."

Valley looked disappointed as she listened to Nurse Barnes' plans. "It's no point of you telling me about your date. I don't have anywhere to write it down. They still haven't given me Johntu back."

"Don't look so down about that, Honey. Sometimes situations can turn in your favor. Take a look in there and tell me what you see..."

Nurse Barnes and Valley were now standing beside Valley's room. Valley peeked in and saw her diary sitting on her desk like it had never left. Valley squealed in delight and then planted a big kiss on Nurse Barnes in appreciation.

"Now be good like I said, and I'll have a juicy story for you when I work my next shift."

Valley nodded her head and then made her way to the desk.

It'd been several months since Valley's last outburst where she tackled a resident for stealing her chair by the window looking out at the courtyard. As part of her punishment, orchestrated by the illustrious Dr. Sumpter, Johntu was taken away from her room to be returned after an undetermined amount of time. Since she'd been on her best behavior for a while, Dr. Sumpter must have agreed to let her have some of her privileges back. The one thing she was looking forward to getting was her journal, Johntu, or just John for short.

She began writing in John when she went to the University and found that writing was a very good comfort; unlike listening to the voices that always wanted her to do wrong, and then would blame her when things didn't go as planned. John was a true companion and spent time with her in places Big Black couldn't go. Others saw him as a diary, but for Valley, it was within his pages that she unfolded her love affair with Ramses. John held all of her secrets, and all of the promises she made for herself and her future with her lover, Ramses.

John also held the deep dark blackness that clouded her mind sometimes. The blackness was hard to endure, but John helped her work through it. With him as her confidant, she could take out her pain on him by writing hard through the pages— ripping through them as she struck the feeble paper with her pen. Seeing the slash marks she made on the pages of her journal mimicked the slash marks on her body made with her trusty blade she kept hidden within John... another secret he held for her. Unfortunately, when she was imprisoned in her current residence for actions she was being held accountable for, the authorities lost the original John, never to be seen again. Valley believed the whole ordeal of him going missing was a conspiracy the doctors and her mother contrived because he was her closest friend. Valley knew that once they got their hands on John they would know all her thoughts in an effort to use against her, and she didn't like it.

In the past, she sometimes felt like John wanted to be found by someone else, so he could escape from her just like Ramses tried to leave her for another woman... a woman who didn't cut him and keep him away from others like she'd done. John probably left her while she was fixated on Ramses and told all of her secrets by opening his pages like a common whore opens her legs. John had betrayed her once he disappeared by telling her deepest and most repressed thoughts, but as relationship goes, she forgave him just like she'd done Ramses.

Now, inside a place she didn't know, with people she didn't want to be around, she'd been granted the privilege of having another journal, Johntu. The relationship between Valley and Johntu had been forged, but it wasn't the same as her and John's. Reluctantly, she had to make due with the new type of relationship she created with Johntu if she wanted someone to talk to. This time however, she wasn't going to tell her new friend as much as she told John. She'll talk in code, and twist her words and thoughts up as she wrote so he wouldn't understand, but just listen to her through her pen. She also found she couldn't strike Johntu like she struck John because he might leave as well. She did find that just ripping the corners of his pages, or letting the pen bleed through his thin insides provided him a hint of what she and John went through.

By comparison, writing in Johntu wasn't the same as writing in John, but it beat having to play scrabble in the smelly recreation room with the drooling old lady with no teeth. Valley hated looking at the dried saliva in the corners of her mouth, and having to smell her bad breath; that lady was a talker and it irritated her to no end listening to her ramble on and on about nothing. Life was just better sitting in her room on the cold laminate flooring, writing in her journal.

Overlooking all of his faults, Johntu was a great listener, and today he was going to get an earful.

9/2012

Can you believe this? Can you actually believe that he walked out on us?! I bet you if I were out of this place, I would show him that it's not wise to walk out on me. First of all, he comes to see me... he wants to see me! I don't want to see him, but I allow him to see me since I know that's what he wants to do. Does he think I like him asking personal questions? No! I don't like people judging me and asking me questions about me or my man, but I let him do it because he likes it. I bet you he really wants me to talk about the time my sexy man fucked me so hard in my ass that it made me sore. See, I would have told him all about it too 'cause I know that's what he really wants to hear. It's funny... I find him kind of hot when he's all squeamish around me at our meetings, like he's waiting for the perfect time to give it to me good. I bet, if I would have told him about me getting fucked in my ass behind that dirty building across the street from the school, it would have made his dick so hard, it would have put a hole right through those ugly khakis he wears! Yeah. I can tell he wants to put his dick in my ass, but he's not going to be able to because I'll break it off if it ever gets close to me! My ass belongs to Ramses!

I have to calm down John. That little crybaby bitch doctor always makes me so upset. I wish he didn't leave our session so early today. Now, he'll come back sooner than usual. He'll be back to ask more of the same damn questions. Hasn't he caught on yet? I only let him ask me stuff because he liked me. Now he doesn't like me, so now I don't like him. I won't be answering anymore questions... he blew it.

Valley wrote a little more before she heard the faint sound of ringing getting louder, and louder. Valley looked around her semi barren room but couldn't see the source of it. The high-pitched ringing became louder. It sounded like it was coming from the bed. Valley cautiously crept on her knees toward the sound. She pulled back the sheets, she placed her ears on the pillows, and then threw all of her bedding on the floor because the sound was not coming from them.

The ringing got louder. It sounded like it was under the mattress. Valley pushed the mattress off of its box spring with all of her strength, but didn't see the ringing's source. Valley was getting frustrated with the high-pitched noise. The ringing was becoming louder and steadier. Valley started panicking thinking that it was some outer force signaling that her time was up... that her life was over... that she was next to die like she'd always predicted by the hands of her mother. She continued looking around the room in search of the deafening ring. Her breathing became harder. She needed something... something to make the ringing stop, but there was nothing available for her to use. All she could do was pace the floor holding her hands tightly to her ears.

More minutes passed as Valley tried to hold it together, but the noise made her heart race. There was an unpleasant tightness in her chest from all the stress the sound caused. She sat in the corner holding her ears firmly. Her chest hurt. Her palms sweated. She anxiously wiggled her foot as she thought of what to do. All the while, the ringing felt incessant. She was out of control. She couldn't stop the ringing. She bit her bottom lip as she closed her eyes. The ringing continued. She bit down harder. The ringing was louder. She forced her teeth to break the skin on her lip. There was pain. She felt the blood on her tongue. The ringing continued.

Finally a decrescendo happened. The volume of the ringing started to fade as the blood from her lip came faster. Valley continued to vigorously bite down assured that her actions were what made the ringing cease. Finally, the room was silent. She let her teeth release her bottom lip. Her hands dropped to her side. She stood from the corner she'd backed herself in, and licked the blood from her wound.

She sat back down on the cool laminate floor and picked up her journal like nothing just happened, and began to write.

Johntu. I know it was you. You were the one who started the ringing. I should have known it was you. I'm listening now. What do you want from me? Do you want me to be honest with you, and tell you everything like I told John? What do you want me to do? Do you want me to cut? I can't cut myself anymore. They took my knife from me. They took my Ramses from me too. I have nothing. What do you want me to do?

The ringing suddenly came back louder and stronger. It was faster and more painful; pounding at her temples for all of her attention. She grabbed her ears once more and screamed out in pain. The ringing was now coming from everywhere in the room. Valley was manic trying to find a way to stop the ringing. She went to her desk and began going through her drawers throwing paper after paper. She then went back to the bed and flipped it on its side, enraged that the ringing disconnected her from the voices, which were her only hope in becoming calm in her state of chaos. Before she could continue on her path of destruction, the nurses were in her room trying to restrain her from doing any more damage. Valley screamed out, "You all are doing this to me! I thought it was John, but it is YOU! Stop the ringing! Stop the ringing! Stop the ringing!"

The nurses looked at each other in confusion, but continued to handle her with as much force as they could. Then, as soon as the ringing began, it stopped. All was quiet. Sound slowly came back to her, and she could hear the nurses trying to quiet her down. She looked at them with a blank stare. She stood still while they checked her over for any scars or anything that would have set her off but they didn't find anything. One nurse put Valley's bed back together while another put her desk in order. The nurse attending to Valley couldn't find anything wrong with her, and asked, "Are you okay? Do you know why you were screaming?"

Valley looked at her and shook her head no. The nurse led her to the bed and placed her between its covers. "Baby, you gotta pull it together. How do you expect to get out of here if you acting like this?"

Valley looked at the nurse and saw who she wanted to see most of all. She smiled a glossed over love smile at the female nurse who resembled Ramses in a most hallucinative way. The words she thought he said to her were assuring... *"He still loves me"*. Valley thought to herself as she nodded her head slowly at the nurse's request.

"Anything for you. All things I do, I do for you. I love you so much." Tears welled in Valley's eyes and then streamed down her face. The nurse put the covers over her body, and then leaned in to fluff her pillow. Valley grabbed the nurse by her neck, and forced their mouths together while slipping her tongue down the woman's throat.

The nurse was shocked and began to struggle to free herself from the patient. Once she did, she wiped her mouth with her sleeve.

"Valley! What has gotten into you?!"

Valley mouthed the words, "I love you too", and then rolled over to fall asleep— exhausted from the whole ordeal.

"Nurse Ann... what was that about?"

"I don't know..."

"I know it's your first week here, but does she know you to kiss you like that?"

"Oh gosh, no! I only met her today."

"Well, something got into her to kiss you like that."

"Well, I sure don't want it to happen again. I think I need to put in for a transfer."

CHAPTER FIFTEEN

Valley put Big Black back in his velvety cloth sack and slid her blade back into the pages of John. She neatly stacked her dildo on top of her diary, and then placed them both in a petite ornate trinket box she got from her father while on a treasure hunt at the flea market. She closed the chest's lid, locked it, and then pushed it underneath her bed to the furthest upper corner. She then hurriedly placed the junk that she pulled from underneath her bed to get to the locked treasure chest back to its scrambled position under the bed to once again hide her little secret.

This was the first time in a month or so that she had to pull them both out to pleasure herself, but it was necessary due to the anxiety she had walled up inside of her. Recently there'd been a lack of sexual encounters between Giselle and Ramses, and the older stories she used to get her ready for her romps with Big Black had grown stale.

She checked the room once more for any clues that would call attention to the lurid act she just performed on herself— igniting her freshly cut skin on the candle that burned on her dresser, while she rode Big Black, and moaning Ramses name, all while watching the climax scene of a porn video would cause anyone to question her sanity. As a precautionary measure, Valley sprayed air freshener and then opened the window just a crack to ventilate the room. Giselle could literally sniff out anything, and some things in Valley's life Giselle was just not privy too.

More relaxed and ready for a new date night story (if there was going to be one), Valley flipped on the little television that sat on her dresser to zone out to the soothing voice of Bob Ross, the artist on the Public Broadcasting Station show, "Joy of Painting". Valley hypnotically watched him make happy little clouds on the canvas as she listened out for the familiar jiggle of the door handle. Valley didn't have to wait long before she heard Giselle's key turn in the lock.

"Oh… hey Valley… I didn't know you were going to be here… I'll just get some things and head over to a friend's house for the night." Giselle rushed to put her books down and then to pull her overnight bag from the top shelf of her closet.

Valley sat up on the bed stunned. *"It's only Wednesday… she has class tomorrow. Who would she be staying with tonight?"*

Valley turned off the television as she tried to look casual. "You aren't bothering me. You can stay if you like." Valley watched Giselle place a pair of jeans and a t-shirt in her bag before she went back into her closet to find a pair of sneakers to match.

"So, do you have an all night study session, or do you have a big date with your guy friend, Ramses?"

"Huh? Oh, no… I'm just going to chill with this new girl I met in class." Giselle came out of the closet with a pair of hightop Converse that looked as if she were wearing a graffiti wall on her feet. She placed the pair of shoes in the backpack and then started rummaging on top of her dresser for her jewelry.

"That sounds fun. Do you mind if I tag along?" Valley got off the bed and went to her dresser to begin pulling out something to wear. Valley heard Giselle's shuffling stop.

With doubt in her voice, Giselle responded, "Valley, I don't think it's a good idea if you come along. Chica doesn't know you."

"Wow, that's never stopped you from inviting me before."

Giselle looked down in embarrassment. It was really the first time she'd brushed her best friend off to hang with someone new.

"We usually go everywhere together. What's the deal Giz? It's like you've been avoiding me."

Giselle sat on Valley's bed, and patted the space beside her indicating she wanted Valley to sit down for a heart-to-heart.

"Valley, it's true. I have been avoiding you. Frankly, you've been creeping me out ever since the orgy."

Valley's eyes widened and her cheeks turned red from mortification.

Giselle rubbed Valley's knee empathetically because her words were prone to come out harsh and blunt. "Now don't take what I'm saying the wrong way. I still love you... you are still *one* of my friends, but I think we have grown apart. We haven't been on campus that long, and I have explored new horizons, discovered new worlds, and been involved with mature people who appreciate things like good wine, great art, and amazing sex. I've grown up, and you can't seem to handle adult themed entertainment like I can." Finished with her assessment, Giselle paused satisfied that she'd done such a great job letting her friend down easy. Ready to go, Giselle grabbed her things from off her dresser and tossed them in the bag.

"I'm sorry if I spazzed out on you in front of your friends. Can I be honest with you? The orgy was my first time having sex ever. I was just a little scared is all."

"I knew you were still a virgin!" Giselle squealed and laughed a little bit as she jumped up and down while clapping her hands. "I can't believe you got your cherry popped at an ORGY!!!" Giselle giggled hysterically until she doubled over the bed laughing.

Valley was ashamed to admit the truth, but wanted to desperately keep their friendship... it was the only way to continue her relationship with Ramses.

"Don't laugh Giselle. It was so overwhelming for me, but I thought I did a good job keeping my cool. Hey... why don't you set up another date with your friends so I can get some more practice?"

Giselle was now composed and back at gathering her things; ready to leave for the evening.

"That's all fine and good Valley, but they weren't feeling you anyway. Ramses couldn't believe you were the friend that was supposed to be so sexy and down for whatever, and Chad was pissed when you blew him off at the elevator. And then... the whole barking thing? What was that about? You really were a total flake that night." She took one more look around the room, before leaving, but then held up her pointer finger as she remembered one other subject she wanted to bring up. She turned back to Valley and had sufficed that she had to mention it before she left for the evening. "I've also been meaning to talk to you about your hygiene. I mean... you have really let yourself go! Your nasty hair, that stinky body of yours, and your ungodly breath! How can you stand your own self?! The shower stalls aren't that full, Val. You could wash more often if you really wanted to." With that, Giselle picked up her pocketbook and her book bag off the floor, and threw her overnight bag across her body.

As Giselle reached for the door, Valley panicked that she would lose her best friend and her man if she didn't stall her.

"Giselle... I didn't know I was that bad! I promise I'll take more showers... I'll be better in bed the next time! Tell them I've been practicing!"

"Save it Val. I'm not even seeing Ramses anymore." Giselle proclaimed unapologetically.

"What?! You were just with him a couple of weeks ago!"

"Yeah, well we're over. I'm seeing someone else now... You've seen him. He plays on the basketball team. I just love climbing up his long legs to get on that pole."

Valley's jaw had dropped. Her world was crushed. *He's broken up with me! What could I have done that was so bad?!*

"Damn Val, Don't look so shocked! You look more broke up about it than I did!" Giselle giggled again, and left out the room, shutting the door behind her.

Two seconds later, Giselle stuck her head back in the room only to see Valley still standing there with her mouth open. "And crack a window in here... your pussy stink. Eck!"

CHAPTER Sixteen

Giselle's revelation made Valley uneasy. She never thought of them being broken up. All of the good times she's had with the man of her dreams were now gone— and she didn't even know why. Valley sat on her bed and looked out of the window. She saw Giselle walk pass with her new friends. They were laughing as young women did while they made their way to the apartments off campus.

Valley wished she would have been invited. If only those girls knew that she was just as fun as her spunky friend. If only Giselle had introduced her as a cool chick they could "kick it" with instead of agreeing with them that she wasn't good enough to be around, she too would have been included in the movie nights, the pillow fights, and the gossip time. Had Giselle kept her promise about looking out for her when they got to campus, she wouldn't be the girl in love with a guy who barely paid her any attention. The isolation she created meant no one at Virginia University understood her. No one got her brand of uniqueness. She was special, and she had the capacity to be a big hit amongst her peers, but she was too shy to shine and missed a lot of opportunities because of it.

Only one person in Richmond understood her. One person was as close to her heart and knew who she really was. One person made her glow, and made her feel beautiful. Ramses was that person; even though it was not visible to the people around them. He changed her in so many ways. From the first time they met on The Quad at Union, to the last time they made love in the back closet at his job. Ramses knew all about her. There was a reason he broke their relationship off. It was clear that there was something she'd done to change his mind about her. It was up to her to figure it out and make it better.

So many reasons as to why he called off their relationship rushed to Valley's head at once, that she had a hard time focusing in on them. As she thought over each of the possible breakup scenarios, she drew her bottom lip in, used her tongue to find a fleshy spot on her thin rose colored flesh, and then began to press her teeth into it. Valley let out a winch from the pain when she realized what horrific activity she started. Biting her lip was something she used to do in her past when she was deep in thought, and mom said it was a very bad habit. She quickly withdrew her teeth and let her lip pop back in place. She hastily got out a Kleenex and wiped the blood away.

"I can't sit here and think about this anymore. I have to do something to win him back."

Valley looked at her watch and saw that it was 5:30 in the afternoon. The sun was about to set, but she had enough time to go out and find her lover and beg him to take her back. She grabbed her lightweight sweater, and left her dorm room.

Outside in the cold autumn air, Valley couldn't decipher where to begin. Out of all the time she'd spent with him in her mind, she never took the time to figure out where he lived. Sure, Giselle retold how they snuggled in his bed, and how he'd make a quick stop at the house before they went out, but Valley never paid attention to Giselle's intricate details on the journey there; she assumed once they were truly committed to each other, they'd get a place of their own where she could come visit or possibly stay.

Not knowing which way to begin, Valley decided to start whichever way the wind blew. Heading towards Lombardy Avenue, Valley looked around the boys dorm, but didn't go in... she was too shy to step foot in it. She then headed towards the gym. Seeing a group of girls walking in as she approached, Valley blended right in; succeeding in avoiding the strange looks of her campus peers. Once at the door of the basketball court, Valley scanned the sparse crowd in search of Ramses since the gym was a known hang out for the guys and the girls. Unfortunately for Valley, Ramses wasn't there. As she made her way out of the gym, her eyes set their selves on Chad. Lucky for Valley, she saw him before he saw her. She ducked into the girl's bathroom while he passed, and hurriedly escaped the gym before he realized she was there.

Back out on The Quad, Valley continued onward to Lombardy; trying to remember all the places she'd heard Giselle mention when dating Ramses. Approaching Broad Street, Valley found the DTLR him and Giselle bought matching Nike's from. She spotted the exact pair of white sneakers Giselle gloated about…

"He paid so much money for these, Val! I can tell he really likes me. I got a feeling he's the one!" Giselle's voice echoed in Valley's head as she stared at the white sneakers. She grabbed the shoe and smelled its leather like a hound sniffing for its hunt.

"Excuse me ma'am, can I help you find a shoe today?"

"Um… no." Startled by the salesman's leering stare, she dropped the shoe and ran out of the store and around the corner. Breathing hard, Valley grabbed her chest feeling how fast her heart was beating. She then wiped the sweat from her brow and slowly slid to the ground into a helpless ball. A winded smile from sheer exhilaration passed to Valley's face. *I smelled the shoes! I touched the exact pair he bought me and felt a spark! I can feel it! He's coming back to me for sure. I know he is!*

"Yeah man! The bitches that's going to be there tonight are going to be so fucking hot! "

"Man… Ramses, tonight is going to be off-the-chain!"

Valley heard the chime of the store's front door open. *"That couldn't possibly be Ramses..."* Valley crawled to the front of the store, stood up, and peaked through the window. *"It is him! Oh my goodness! Look at him... he looks a wreck... he misses me."* Valley opened the store's front door just enough to creep in. She darted around clothing racks; listening to Ramses and his friend talk about a big party they were preparing for.

"What time did you plan on getting there tonight?"

"I don't know, I'm gonna hook up with this girl I met first, and then slide down to the party."

"So you gonna meet us there?"

"Yeah, Ramses. Make sure you save some of the ladies for me."

"Listen to you! You will be *just* leaving a broad, and you'll be ready to get another?! Man... your dick is off the chain!"

"I know! The shit's crazy, but I gotta keep a few in the stable for emergency cases."

The two friends got their purchases rung up and were headed out the store. Valley, trying to keep her balance, crouched between the shoe sale rack, fell on both her hands and knees in their direct path.

"Whoah... are you alright Miss Lady?" Ramses helped Valley off of the ground.

The look in Valley's eye must have scared her handsome man because he looked at her strangely... as if he didn't know her. Trying to contain her excitement about them being reunited so unexpectedly, Valley nodded her head vigorously up and down implying that she was in fact okay. Pleased with the strange woman's answer, Ramses flashed her a smile as he assisted in helping Valley find her footing.

"Speak to him! Now is your chance!" But there were no words for her at that moment. Just as Ramses was about to walk pass her, Valley stepped in his way wanting to tell him something— anything to make him stay. She put her hands on his chest just to make sure she had the strength to tell him how much she loved and worshiped him.

"Tell him now, Valley! Tell him you forgive him, and that you want to get back together!"

"You know what... Do I know you?" Ramses stared in her eyes and studied her features. There was something familiar about her but he couldn't place why.

Oh my goodness! He knows me! "Yes, we ummm... had—"

"Excuse me miss, you can't harass our customers like this." The salesman chastised Valley for what appeared to him as her badgering paying customers. "Sir, do you know this woman?"

"No, man." Valley's familiarity dissipated from Ramses when the sales clerk addressed them. "She fell on the floor in front of me, and I helped her up."

"Ma'am, you'll have to leave our store. You aren't allowed to loiter and harass our customers. If you could just step this way, I'll escort you to the door."

"Wait...wait... wait..." Valley tried to plead to the sales clerk that they did know each other, and that she needed to talk to her lover, but it was no use. As the clerk walked the young vagrant to the door, Ramses and his friend breezed right by Valley and the sales clerk.

"Sorry ma'am but if you are not going to buy anything, you'll have to leave. It's company policy." The sales clerk walked her out of the doors, and handed her a few dollars. "Here... this should be enough to get you a sandwich or something."

Valley turned around to face the street to see Ramses and his friend drive off.

"You let him go! You useless idiot! Why did you do that?"

"Shut up, you! You didn't have the guts to stop him from leaving! You are just now speaking up!"

"Quiet! Quiet! Shut Up!" Valley cupped her ears and walked back down to campus. She couldn't take the bickering in her head any more. The two voices hadn't been heard in a long time, but now, over the last few months, it appeared they were back to keep her company.

CHAPTER SEVENTEEN

"Gotta hurry up. Gotta hurry up. Gotta hurry up." Valley picked up her speed as she swiftly walked down the street mumbling the words and her thoughts to herself. On her way back in her room, Valley found a dress to put on sitting on top of a small trash heap out by the curb. She pulled up her red hair which was now oily and slightly filthy from a week's worth of not bathing into a semi-tight bun on the top of her head. Looking at herself in the mirror, she tried to recreate the sultry vision she turned into the night she and Ramses made real love. Valley felt beautiful and proud of her transformation. In reality, her lipstick was smeared on, the dress was almost a worn out rag, and the heels she had on were run over, bent down in the back sneakers. She grabbed her purse and headed out the building towards the direction of the party which was in The Fan district— at least three miles from Union's campus. The night's autumn breeze was cool but not intolerable as Valley made her way to her destination. She huddled up in her jacket and moved at a swift pace on Broad Street and then onto nearby side streets; keeping the glance of her eye close to the ground as she moved along.

"You think seeing him at the party is going to make him come back to you? Think again... you aren't what he wants!"

"Shut up, bitch! You are always talking to me about what he doesn't want! I know what he wants! He wants me! I know what he wants!"

"You don't know! If you did, you wouldn't step foot in that party to embarrass him! Don't make a fool out of yourself! Turn around and go home!"

"No, no, no, no, no! Leave me alone!" Valley banged her fist against her head with hopes of shutting them up before she entered the party. People who walked past her on the sidewalks saw her beating herself with her fists, but they weren't affected. Most people running around The Fan were known to have a few screws loose.

For months, Valley had listened to the voices berate her about Ramses. She'd grown tired of them and wished they would just be quiet so she could think things through. "In honesty you guys... I know what you're trying to do, but it's not going to work! I love him! Not YOU!"

Valley picked up her pace as she got closer to her destination. Approaching the front door, she sensed a panic within herself...

"You can't go in there! Look at all those people hanging around the front door! Can you imagine how many people are inside having a good time?! Valley, you won't stand a chance in there! Look what you have on!"

"Shut up, you! I look good! I look good!" Valley hit the side of her head once again, as she shouted in disgust. The crowd outside of the house party watched as Valley struggled with her inner voices.

"Yo! Who invited the freak!" A random guy in the crowd shouted out the insensitive comment making everyone turn their attention to Valley. She noticed the interest she'd brought to herself and stopped banging her fist against her temple. The small crowd laughed at her. Not knowing what they were exactly laughing at, Valley insecurely laughed along all while making her way inside the house.

CHAPTER Eighteen

"Now Doc, I want to apologize for my bad behavior last time. I already know that I was wrong for acting a damn fool. Do you forgive me Doc? Do you believe my apology?"

Doctor Sumpter watched Valley as she walked around her side of the room. She moved at a slow pace from one wall to the next; concentrating on placing one foot directly in front of the other. Valley kept her head lowered allowing her red stringy hair to hang below her shoulders. Compared to the stark white room and Valley's stark white resident's uniform, her hair was the only bright spot to be seen.

"Valley, I haven't heard your apology. I heard you say you want to apologize, but I did not hear you apologize."

"Doc, don't be so technical. You know what I meant."

"Valley, you have to say what you mean. You can't say you want to apologize and not say the apology."

"Well, then I apologize." Valley stopped walking around the room, faced Doctor Sumpter, and bowed from her waist. The gesture was a sarcastic one and only given to overemphasize how little his feelings meant to her.

"Now that I have officially apologized, would you please be my friend again?"

"Our relationship is not built on friendship, Valley. I am your doctor, and you are my patient. That is all I can be to you."

"Come on Doc. Be my friend: I don't have any here, and no one but you visits. I think it's only appropriate that we be friends. Besides, I'm all alone in this world… abandoned yet again."

"You aren't alone Valley. Until recently, your mother has come several times to visit you."

"Oh she has? I don't recall that stuck-up contumelious BITCH coming to visit." Valley leaned against the white wall as she thought about her mother, and the dislike she'd grown accustomed to have for her.

Contemplating the years of fervent hate, Valley decided it was the best time to let the doctor in on her true feelings for Shaundra. "You know, she's the reason why I'm here. It started with her lack of sincerity for my well being, and that pompous stick up her ass! "

"Valley, why is there so much aggression towards your mother?"

"She's a bitch that's why." Valley finally chose to sit down in her chair facing Dr Sumpter to have the long needed chat about her monster of a parent.

"Has she done something to you in the past? Would you like to talk about the history of your anger towards her?"

"What anger? There's no anger towards that soulless harlot! She feels nothing, so I feel nothing. I can see talking about her with you is useless."

"Well, I would like to delve into the anger you obviously display when the topic of your mother comes up."

Valley stretched out her legs and folded her arms, staring defensively at the Doctor. The silence that separated the two clued him that he wasn't going to get the answers he wanted by confronting her directly.

"Fine. Let's not talk about your mother. Let's talk about the next best thing... How well do you remember your father?"

"I remember dad very well. He was the love of my life." Valley slid her legs back to create a lap her arms could rest in. "My dad was the best dad ever. He was the bright spot of my day, and kept the queen of mean at least tolerable."

"So your dad was your protector against your mother? Why did you need protection from her?"

"You know why Doc. You've met her." Valley retorted matter-of-factly before she continued.

"Because... she tried to spew her sadistic, religious, overzealous views on me! She wanted *ME* to turn into *HER!* Isn't that crazy, Doc!? Me... be her!? We don't even look alike!" Valley let out a cynical laugh.

"And your dad must have been the one who let you be yourself."

Valley let out a breath of her anger to calm herself before she began again. "Yeah. I was happy with my dad. He took me everywhere and let me do anything I wanted. I wasn't even a bad girl, Doc. I was a really good kid... did everything I was supposed to, made good grades, and stayed out of trouble, but for mommy, it was never good enough."

Talking with the Doctor made Valley revert to her childhood. The conversation made her vulnerable, and Dr. Sumpter took this time to dig deeper in hopes of finding what triggered her disorder.

"What would you have liked from your mother Valley?"

"I just wanted my mommy to play with me. I wanted her to make me cookies, and take me for ice cream. When I was a little girl, mommy would do those things, but then it changed. She acted like she didn't love me."

"When did it all change for you? Do you remember what happened to make your mother so distant?"

"Not really. She just changed after daddy passed away."

From reading her records, Dr. Sumpter knew her father's health failed at a young age, and Valley was left to live with her mother alone in a new state, and without any friends. From the picture Shaundra painted, Valley was a violent adolescent long before her father passed and she'd tried everything to keep her under control, but nothing seemed to work.

"Do you think his death had anything to do with her change in how she acted towards you?"

"Umm....let me think." Valley tapped her pointer finger on her folded in lips as she thought about the question.

"Probably Doc. Mom was pretty mean before then with all the punishments and everything, but she started cussing and drinking a lot when he died. And one time, after daddy died, she spanked me just because I spilled my juice on accident."

"I guess it was a bad time for you guys."

"Yeah." Valley grew solemn. The load of the conversation weighed heavy like a blanket all over her; making the cold feeling of being alone come back. Goose bumps ran up her arms as she fought back her repressed tears. Valley's head was lowered, and her eyes fluttered to a close as she thought back on her childhood.

"That was the moment things got worse. Her abuse was when I started to feel all alone. I remember you, Dr. Sumpter."

Doctor Sumpter's eyes widened as he listened to his finally coherent patient speak in clarity about what was really going on. He'd waited for this moment of recognition, and it was finally before him. He listened intently as Valley continued her monologue.

"I remember the first time my foster family bought me to you, and I remember our last meeting in your office. That was one of the best days of my life... we ate chocolate cake that day." Valley smiled to herself at the thought of a younger Dr. Sumpter sitting across from her at his desk and eyeing her admiringly.

"I have cherished those moments for so long. I'm glad to see you came for me." Valley meant her sentiments about her dear friend, Dr. Sumpter. Underneath all that she had become, she was still that little girl who got a really bad deal.

Listening to her innocence, Dr. Sumpter nodded his head approvingly.

"But Doc... I know I was messed up before her. I remember the awful things I used to do when I was younger and living in the group homes. What happened to me before I went to live with my parents?"

Doctor Sumpter almost fell out of his seat as he rushed towards the glass that separated them from each other. He put one hand on the window in desperation; scanning his patient with his eyes... awed that she was in fact mentally present.

"I should have told you before." The doctor spoke his words sorrowfully towards Valley. "I should have told you about where I found you and what I put you through before it came to this."

Valley looked at him with question in her eyes. He was about to continue with his confession, but there was something else he saw when he looked at her. Her eyes began to move slowly from left to right, but then rapidly from side to side as she tried to process whatever she was thinking.

Valley's brow frowned. She looked menacing and continued talking never once acknowledging Dr. Sumpter's revelation. "Then she took me away from you. I knew we were leaving and I was never going to see you again. I was okay with that because I had my father, but then he fell ill. He got sick. They want me to believe it was sudden cardiac arrest, but I know it wasn't. I know my mother made it happen."

Valley's moment of clarity where Dr. Sumpter was going to explain the details of her life was now gone. He was now back to looking in the eyes of a crazed woman.

Her dissention into madness had started once again. Valley's breathing picked up. She dug her fingers into the palms of her folded hands as hard as she could. The pain she caused herself made her intensified mood grow. She felt powerful as she prepared her next statement.

"She is a murderer! She is the one who should be here and NOT me!" Valley rose from her seat and picked up the chair, flinging it at the Plexiglas partition.

"She should be here WITH me!"

Dr. Sumpter stumbled away from the window and ran out the room.

"She killed my father! She killed my soul! I hate her for what she has done!" Valley pounded the glass with her fist. She heard the buzzer for the exit door. Valley made a run for the door in an attempt to escape from the confining facility. Instead, she saw the orderly's with their restraints rush into her side of the room. "NO! I DON'T WANT TO GO BACK IN THERE!" Valley shrieked and cried as she begged to be left alone. "NO, PLEASE! DON'T PUT ME BACK IN THAT ROOM! LET ME OUT OF HERE! I CAN'T TAKE IT ANYMORE! SOMEONE HELP

ME!" The nurses gathered around her as she thrashed violently to keep them at bay. Her red hair flung wildly around making it harder for the nurses to hold her still as they attempted to control one of their worst patients.

Dr. Sumpter, out of breath and shaken by what he'd just experienced, watched from the other side of the room. Defeat was all that could come to mind as he listened to her beg for her freedom. *"She's never going to be well. She's gone forever."* Unlike his usual sentiments about his patient, Dr. Sumpter's thoughts were sympathetic and heartfelt about her well being.

Dr. Sumpter turned to a nurse that came to peek into the room and find out what all the commotion was about. He placed his hand gently on her shoulder to get her attention.

"Nurse, please inform the board that my time here is done. I will no longer be able to treat Ms. De'Amore. Her mental state is far beyond my professional experience.

"Yes, Dr. Sumpter." The nurse said understandingly.

As he made his way down the hall, Dr. Sumpter looked back towards the nurse who'd turned her interest back to the demented young woman, and said, "I will clean out my desk and send them a letter resigning myself from her care."

Empathetic to his decision, the nurse replied, "Yes, Dr. Sumpter." while she shook her head and smiled patiently.

CHAPTER NINETEEN

It was a warm Saturday… unusually warm for a spring day. The funeral parlor on the upscale end of Patterson Avenue was full to capacity of family and friends wishing to pay their respects to the pillar of the west end community. Jack De'Amore was adored, cherished, and loved by all who made his acquaintance. It was tragic that his life was taken so soon; leaving a wife, and a young daughter who depended on him for his generous love and affection.

The funeral was elaborate. Flowers for the deceased bombarded the alter and overflowed the aisles. Shaundra sat stoically on the first row with her head held high; daring herself to show an ounce of undignified mourning as a dutiful wife. Shaundra was a picture of pure perfection as she waited for the service for her husband to begin. It was purposefully being held up in hopes that their teenage daughter Valley would show up to honor her father with a last prayer of remembrance.

The crowd was anxious to begin. The handheld fans had all been passed out, and the air conditioning unit burned out not too long after the service should have started.

"Mrs. De'Amore, we truly want to respect the honor of your husband, but we've been waiting for young Miss Valley for quite some time. For the sake of the service not being rushed through, it would be best to start now."

Shaundra cut her eyes at the pastor for suggesting that they begin burying her husband without her daughter being present. "My daughter will be here. She's having a hard time dealing with the sudden death of her father. I assumed you'd understand how delicate this situation is, and wouldn't mind waiting for a child who is obviously grieving."

"My apologies for my inconsiderate suggestion. I just didn't want your husband's guests to suffer through the uncomfortable heat."

Clenching her anger between her teeth, Shaundra answered the pastor as best she could. "Their discomfort in my child's hour of bereavement is of no concern of mine. I have paid top dollar to bury my husband with dignity and class. You will wait for my child, and the service will not start a minute before she gets here."

Suddenly the doors of the funeral home flew open. Shaundra and all of the funeral guests turned their attention to the figure standing in the middle of the entrance. The sunlight poured in from behind the thin intruder draped in white sheaths. As the figure moved down the aisle, the doors of the parlor closed behind them; allowing Shaundra to see who'd entered.

"Oh dear God!" Shaundra held her head in shame as Valley walked up to her and placed a kiss on the top of her hair. Valley made her way to the podium and stood before the crowd with a shaven head and covered in white powder all over. Valley looked like a ghost. Her green eyes more visible than ever against her all white face. Her lips glossed shiny red.

"People, friends, and family." Valley paused and looked towards her mother and smiled as Shaundra looked up at her from her pew. "There is a truth that has been cloaked in lie. The reality has been kept buried deep inside our picture perfect home never to be told.

This truth was to lay dormant forever as it would have been buried with my dearly departed father."

"Valley! Come from that podium right this minute!" Shaundra stood up as she demanded that Valley come to take a seat beside her.

Valley calmly smiled at her mother and shook her head no. "Mother, you are worried that I've found out the truth, and you should be." Valley turned her attention back to the crowd as she continued. "For the time has come to reveal your sinister plan!" Valley pointed an accusatory finger in her mother's direction as she spoke. "You have gotten away with the murder of my father, but you will not get away with the murder of me!"

Shaundra gasped in horror, and then fainted as Valley's accusation came down on her with all their friends and family present. The crowd was in awe at the spectacle, and a low murmur rose from the crowd as Valley slandered her own mother's character.

"My mother, and her greedy lifestyle, found the map to the hidden treasure in our basement! My father only told me about it, but she found the map had been hid for safe keeping!" Valley held up a hand drawn map that was done in colored markers and crayons as if a child had created it during play time.

"I stand before you cloaked in a force field to protect myself from Shaundra's evil powers! Had I come unprotected to bid my father farewell, I would have perished in the way of my father, whose insides were disintegrated from my mother's touch!"

Valley raised her hands before the crowd as a minister would do to praise God's good graces.

"People, hear me now! Gather together to rid the world of my mother, or you will be next to die by her hand!"

The room was quiet as she left the podium. With her hands still raised, she stood at the bottom of the pulpit where her father's casket lay open.

"For the love of my father! I shall take my own life in honor of his valor! This potion I shall drink will cleanse my soul as it kills me instantly! I'd rather die by my own hand than to wait for my mother to satisfy her quest for blood!"

Valley snatched the vile hanging from her neck and drank the red elixir inside of it. A shriek came from the crowd as Valley began to choke. She clutched her neck in panic and finally fell across her father's body.

"Someone get her to the hospital!" Someone from the pews yelled. The pastor grabbed Valley from the casket and rushed her outside to the ambulance that stayed in the parking lot during services.

"Get her to the hospital immediately! She said she drank something poisonous!" Frantically the ambulance took off; arriving at the hospital in no time.

After coming out of her fainting spell, Shaundra reached the hospital twenty minutes later looking worn out from all the commotion her daughter had caused.

"Nurse, my daughter was bought in here not too long ago for drinking poison. Is she okay? Which room is she in?" Shaundra looked down the dissected hall trying to predict which direction she should head in search of Valley.

"She's sitting in the waiting room ma'am. She's just fine."

Shaundra turned around and saw Valley sitting behind her in the lobby watching the television.

"No you must be mistaken. She drank poison at her father's funeral. She said it would kill her instantly."

"Ma'am... she drank red kool-aid. We gave her something to throw up the contents of her stomach, and they figured all she drank was red kool-aid. She's fine to go home." The nurse turned her attention back to her computer and began clicking away on the keyboard.

"That little bitch! I can't believe she did this to me!" Shaundra pounded her fist on the nurses' station frustrated that her daughter had taken her through such turmoil.

"Excuse me?" The nurse was stunned by the woman's reaction to her daughter's condition.

Immediately regaining her demeanor, Shaundra turned her attention back to the nurse and smiled. "Please excuse my choice words. It has been a very long day. My daughter has given us a fright with her anecdotes. She has a history of medical illness, and I believe she would be best suited staying here until she is under control."

"Ma'am, paperwork will need to be filled out, and she is of age to refuse medical treatment. If she doesn't feel she needs medical assistance for her mental state, you can request Social Services to be involved, and they will need to determine if she is mentally unstable and harmful to herself and others."

"I understand. No need to worry with all of that. I will have all the paperwork ready to go and she'll be ready for admittance on tomorrow."

"Ma'am, there is a process that takes about a week to complete. The earliest she'll be able to be admitted is Monday after next.

"Don't worry about that. She'll be here tomorrow to receive the best care this hospital has to offer."

Shaundra walked away from the nurses' station and into the waiting room.

"Valley. Come along dear. We have a funeral to finish attending. Our guest are waiting."

"Coming mother." Valley welcomed her mother's presence by giving her a hug and then grabbed Shaundra's hand to leave; waving happily at the nurse who watched them exit the hospital.

CHAPTER TWENTY

"Two hours and no Ramses. He said he was going to be here. He said he would be here... on time and ready to apologize to me, and he is not here. He told me to dress up... I put this outfit on just for him and now it's riding up my legs trying to expose my butt... I need a drink. Oooh! There's a drink. I'll just take this and go stand in the corner and wait for him. Yeah... I'll just stand right here in this spot 'cause he'll be looking for me when he walks through the door. Yup. I'm positive he'll be here soon. Wait...why are people looking at me? Do I have something on my dress?" Valley turned around and around like a dog chasing its tail as she tried to find the messy spot people were obviously staring at. After scrutinizing her appearance the best way she knew how, she couldn't find anything wrong with her attire. She looked back at them agitated that she was the one chosen to be ostracized.

"What are these crazy people looking at?"

"They're staring at you! We told you it was a bad idea to come to the party! You were not invited!"

Defensively, Valley curved her body like a cat waiting to pounce on her prey as she watched them watch her. She crept back into the corner keeping her eyes on the people that appeared to be looking at her. She hunched her shoulders and arched her back more as she prepared for what seemed like an attack from the crowd.

"Stop looking at me– all of you. Turn away!" Valley spat the words out and screwed her face in anger at the peering eyes.

"Man... something is definitely wrong with that chick! Again... who let in the freak?!"

Valley turned her back to the laughing crowd that had already begun to disperse into the party atmosphere. Left alone with her face in the corner and sipping on a borrowed drink, Valley was once again by herself waiting on Ramses to walk through the door.

"You are wasting your time. He will not come. He knows you are here and will not come to keep away from you. You plan to do him harm, and he knows it."

"Shut up! You talk like you know him! You don't know him like I do! He'll be here!" In a fit of rage Valley pulled out her knife and sliced her forearm; not caring if anyone saw.

"This is what you want! I gave you what you want! You want to see me in pain! Here is my pain!" Even though her slice was more to satisfy the voices in her head, she needed to see herself bleed more than they did. The affect the open air had on her wound calmed her down, and had officially calmed the voices.

More relaxed, she finished up her drink, and placed the cup on the table as she continued to wait. She then picked up another red plastic cup filled with another type of libation, smelled it, and then gulped it down quickly; throwing the cup and its remnants to the floor.

"Hey... are you okay? You're bleeding..." A thin blonde haired young woman grabbed Valley's arm abruptly to get a better look at the wound. "That's so gross! Hey guys! Look at this! She's got a cut!"

Valley snatched her arm away to hide her slice as a group of the young lady's friends turned to see.

"Don't worry girl, I'm studying to be a medicine something or whatever. I'll take care of you, for sure. Someone get me a band aid STAT! We've got a boo-boo to mend people!" The blonde leaned on Valley as she and her friends laughed at her intoxicated orders. "Oh My God, you guys! I'm going to piss myself! This party ROCKS!" The crowd went up in an overwhelming roar of approval.

Valley took that as her moment to duck away from the commotion, and to clean her arm. Walking up the flight of stairs to the second floor of the house, Valley peeked into the rooms looking for the bathroom.

"Valley! Is that you over there?"

Startled, Valley turned around to see Giselle, and a bunch of her new friends.

"Ohmygaw, girl! I didn't know you were coming! Who are you here with?" Giselle peeped around the 2nd floor hallway trying to spot anyone who may appear to look like the type of person her roommate would hang out with.

"I um, came by myself... I mean... I'm waiting on my friend to show up." Valley awkwardly scratched her leg as she twisted herself around to find her itch.

"I can see you *tried* to get dressed up. You look..." Giselle looked Valley up and down trying to find words to describe the unfortunate mistake in front of her.

"... like you should have never tried getting dressed in the dark." Giselle tried hard to hold in her laughter, but once she let out that one giggle, the rest of them came afterwards. Her friend's also doubled over in laughter; ribbing each other and pointing at the fashion disaster.

"Well, I wanted to try something different... you know me. Always ready for something new." Valley nervously laughed along with them, but couldn't manage the same amount of buoyancy in her voice as they did.

"I um... gotta go pee. I'll see you around." Valley spotted the bathroom, dipped in and cleaned her arm. The cut wasn't that deep so when the cold water hit it, the blood ceased to run. Valley wrapped her wound with some paper towels she found on the sink and left the bathroom; merging with the crowd that stood around in the hallway. Rerouting herself back down the hall, she came back down the stairs only to spot her man held up at the makeshift drink table. Adorned in all white from head to toe, he appeared like a gallant knight ready to take her away and find a quiet spot for them to talk their relationship problems over.

Thinking about how wonderful it would be to grab him by the hand and lead the way to a secluded corner, Valley realized that her feet were moving towards him without her permission— she wasn't ready to make her presence known.

"Stop it feet! Stop, stop, stop! Listen to my commands and stop moving right now!" Valley pounded the side of her legs with her fist as she mumbled the commands to herself.

The thumping pain made her feet obey, and she stood stiff as a board— frozen while in movement through the walkway... eyes glued on Ramses with people forced to walk around her.

Oh God, I need another drink before I do this. Valley thought as she feared the time had finally come for them to reconcile. "Leg's, activate!" Her knees bent and her feet swiftly took off in the opposite direction.

I can't approach him now. I'd make a fool of myself. They were right. I should have stayed home. I should have listened to them. Now in a different room of the house, Valley looked around until she saw another abandoned cup full of the alcoholic punch she'd been enjoying all night. She grabbed it quickly and began gulping it down.

"Hey Lady! That's my drink!" The young man standing beside her shouted out.

Valley darted her eyes towards the guy accusing her of stealing an obviously abandoned cup, and then quickly turned the other way after she crudely stuck her tongue out at him to disappear in the crowd.

The guy looked at her as she took possession of his drink; perplexed as to why she'd been stealing only his drinks all night. In a frustrated huff, he complained out loud, "Why is it every time I come to these things, I get harassed by the ugly chick!"

CHAPTER TWENTY-ONE

"Alright man! Drive safe, yo! I'll holla at ya'll geeks tomorrow." Ramses laughed with his crew as they drove away thinking about their shenanigans at the party. Being the gentleman that he was, he'd made plans to stay and help clean up his partner's home after it had been thoroughly destroyed by the guests.

"My man..." Ramses tapped his friend on his shoulder to point his attention to what he saw. "Who is the chick dancing by herself in the corner? Does she even realize the music has stopped?"

"I'm not sure, dude, but she is *fucked up*!"

Ramses raised his voice just enough to get the young lady's attention. "Yo, Miss! Yo!"

Valley didn't hear the two guys calling out to her. She was too busy practicing her moves for later tonight with Ramses. She was thrown off guard when she felt a hand on her shoulder, and then turning around to see Ramses standing there.

"Yo, Miss Lady. You alright? Did you come here with anyone that can take you home?"

Valley clasped her hands over her mouth in surprise.

"Oh shit! Valley he's right in front of you!"

"Yeah what are you going to do?!"

"Stop talking to me so I can get out of here!"

Valley turned around abruptly to run away from his charming stare, but she didn't realize she was headed for the living room wall.

"Ouch!" Valley slammed right into it head first, and then fell backwards, only to be caught by her lover before she hit the floor.

"Baby girl, you are too smashed to leave here by yourself. Did you come with anyone?"

Half unconscious, Valley looked at Ramses, and replied, "I came here for you..."

"Whoa momma, you must have me confused. The drink must got you twisted." Ramses laughed while waving his hand like a fan over Valley's face.

"Pew! Your breath stinks like you've been drinking for days! I bet you were the one who emptied the keg we had in the kitchen." Ramses laughed once more, putting a dazed smile on Valley's face.

"I love you so much. I just need to know, why did you leave me. Can we please go somewhere and talk about us?"

Ramses shook his head as he looked at the pathetic sight in front of him. "Yo, man. Home girl over here is done. Do you mind if I cut out and take her home? She too drunk to walk back by herself, and it looks like she came here alone."

"Yeah, Ramses. Go on and take her home. I can handle this."

Ramses turned his focus back to the mangy young lady sprawled out in his arms, "Young Miss, you lucked up tonight. Being the gentleman that I am, I'm going to escort you to a safe place. Where would you like to go?"

"Take me home, baby. Take me home with you." Valley replied sleepily.

"Take you home with me? That's not going to happen." Ramses laughed. It appeared to him that he was dealing with a girl who had her "drunk goggles" on and thought he was someone else.

Valley swayed back and forth and from side to side as she stared at Ramses. She loved him so much. Her silly grin full of adoration filled her face from ear to ear.

"Just love me again for old time's sake and I swear I'll be better this time. I'll do you right." Valley reached out to give him a hug, but almost fell to her face in front of him.

"Whoa, Sweetie! With your level of tolerance, you really shouldn't drink!" Ramses caught Valley before she fell; scooping her up in his massive arms.

"Oh, Baby. You're my hero. I knew you still loved me." Valley let out a hiccup and a smelly belch as she wrapped her arms around her savior.

Ramses shook his head, and with a carefree chuckle, he carried Valley to his car.

Hearing the car door slam was very sobering for Valley. She looked up and around the unfamiliar environment; vaguely remembering how she even got there. She stuck her hand out, and felt the nice leather seats of the small sports car as she watched the masculine shadowy figure get in on the driver's side. She was more than surprised to see her man slide Into his seat, and then grab the passenger seat belt to lock her in place.

"Oh, so you're up now. You were knocked out while I struggled to walk those four blocks to the car. It would have been nice if you would have woken up maybe a block or two back." Ramses laughed a little assuring his passenger that she was actually no problem at all.

"Thanks." Valley said bashfully.

"Now is your time Valley! You have him right where you want him! Make your move!"

"Shhhh! Not right now!"

"Did you say something?" Ramses looked at Valley perplexed as he put his key in the ignition.

"I... oh... nothing. Just sort of talking to myself."

"Well, it's okay if you talk to yourself; it's a problem if you respond." Ramses laughed once more as the ignition started.

"Now, that you are a little bit sober, can you please tell me where I can drop you?"

"Yeah...you can just drop me off at the University."

"Do it now before it's too late!"

"Alright! Just wait!"

"Are you still over there talking to yourself? You know I'm sitting right here... you can talk to me if you'd like." Ramses laughed once again as he waited for the car to warm up.

"Well, before we go, I would like to talk to you about something important." Valley was uneasy expressing her undying love, but she had to take advantage of the moment.

"Really... I wasn't expecting you to want to pour your heart out to me, but okay. What's up?"

The words she wanted to say were hard to get out one by one— they were all so congested within thought that she had to blurt them out all at once just so they all could be heard. "I just want to know if I missed my chance to get back with you. I know our break up was abrupt, but don't you think ending our relationship was a bit over the top? We had a lot of good times together."

Ramses stared at her in disbelief for a brief moment, and then let out another hearty laugh. He couldn't believe she still thought he was someone else. "Sweetie, you have been talking to me all night like I'm some guy you know. He and I must really look alike for you to keep mistaking us. Listen, I'm not the— hold on. My phone is ringing." Ramses reached in his pocket and pulled out his phone. He looked at the number, hit the answer button, and put it to his ear.

"Yeah... what's up?"

While Ramses talked on his cellular, Valley found this to be the right opportunity to get her thoughts straight. She went over her plea in her mind as he talked to the person on the other end of his call.

"Hold up let me put you on speaker. I'm about to pull off."

The speaker button was clicked. "So where did you say you were headed?" The voice was mellow and sweet as her sultry tone beckoned for him to come over. It was the other woman.

Valley's temperature escalated as she heard him speak with ease to the one person who stood between them getting back together. *"How could he be talking to that tramp while I'm trying to work things out between us?!"*

"See I told you he didn't want you! You couldn't have possibly believed he was going to be with you!"

"Shut up! Shut up! Shut up!! You don't know what he wants!" Valley began to scream and bang the side of her head against the window in a fit of rage and frustration!

Ramses looked at his passenger not knowing what to do. "Babe, let me call you back. Something's wrong with this chick." Ramses hung up the phone and pulled the car over.

Valley held her aching head in her hands as she wept. Ramses watched what seemed to be a drunken break down. He dared not get any closer to the strange woman because he still hadn't deciphered what ticked her off.

"Look lady, I want to get you back to the dorms or at least to a safe place, but right now you are freaking me out."

Valley wiped her tears with the back of her hand, and stopped her sobbing. Feeling out of control, she stuck her hand in her bag in search of her small pocket knife. She needed to hold the blade tight; as it was her only way of dealing with the tragic situation in front of her.

"Stop acting like you don't know me Ramses. You knew it would hurt me to hear her on the other end of that call, and that's why you put her on speaker. I know we are broken up, but you don't have to flaunt your new girl in front of me like what we had— what we shared didn't matter!"

Valley looked at him with pleading eyes before she started again. "Don't you know you are a part of me?"

"See, this is the type of shit I'm talking about..." Ramses mumbled to himself before he turned to address her. "I'm sorry, but I do not know you. As a matter of fact, how do you know my name?"

Valley laughed at his statement; amused at how far he would go to try and get over her. "Baby, stop playing games. This break up has been just as hard on me as it has been on you, but I'm not going to go as far as to act like I don't know you." Valley reached out to caress the hair that grazed the top of his ear, but he flinched away, and Valley pulled her hand back just as swiftly.

"Look at him Valley. Look at his face. Look at his eyes. You repulse him. He doesn't want you! He's not yours! He's never been yours! He belongs with that girl he was talking with! You'll never have him now!"

"Shut up! Shut up! Shut up! Shut up! Stop talking to me! He loves me and you know it!"

Ramses watched Valley shake her head, and beat her face with her fist as she spoke angrily. He put his hand to his face and slid it down in woe. "I'm officially never helping another drunken bitch as long as I LIVE!"

Ramses got out of the driver's side door and went to the passenger side to open it. "No offense, but I can't deal with this tonight. You are freaking me out with all your crazy talk to me and to yourself. Please get out of my car. I hope you can find your way home safely."

Valley kept her head low as he got out of the car, but finally looked up to him coldly as he insisted that she remove herself. The way her eyes burned into him as he stood there waiting for her to get out sent chills up his arm. Ramses squirmed uncomfortably, and watched her pull her hand out of her bag.

"I want to show you something."

"Just get out of my car."

Valley's hand was clenched tight around her blade. Ramses could only see her blood dripping from between the cracks of her fingers and not the blade she had hidden inside.

"Yo! You're bleeding! What the hell are you holding?!"

Valley opened her hand to expose her black pocket knife with the curved blade covered in her own blood. "I had to show you what you put me through. You do this to me." Valley stuck her other arm out, and placed the blade of the knife on her forearm.

"What the hell are you doing?! Don't do that!" Ramses shrieked in alarm at the sight of the girl sitting in his car slicing on herself.

"Don't worry, honey... it doesn't hurt as much as the painful acts you commit against our love." Valley pushed the knife's blade into her milky white skin. The puncture produced a red spot that began to grow larger as she dug her blade deeper within herself.

Ramses looked on in panic; scared to run for help, but frightened to stay and watch.

"Oh baby, just watching you watch me cut myself is making me cum... Cutting is so sacred... I never thought I could share a moment like this with you." Valley smiled slyly and let the blade run down her arm. "This is the deepest I've ever cut before... I love it..."

The back of Ramses' legs ached with empathy as Valley did her damage. His knees almost buckled at the sight of how much she enjoyed mutilating herself. For the sake of getting a good night's sleep, Ramses couldn't take anymore of the skinny white girl moaning in ecstasy while wounding her body. He reached into the car to grab the blade from the crazy cutter, but she was too quick.

"Don't make me do this to you Ramses!" She sliced his cheek suddenly as a warning. Ramses felt the effects of her handy work as the cold breeze hit the wound.

"I love you, but if you ever grab for my blade again, you WILL die." Valley meant her words.

"Bitch, play time is over. Get the fuck out of my car right now!"

"Tell me who she is."

"None of your got-damn business! Get out of my car!"

"You love her!"

"Fuck you! Get out!"

"Did you make her swallow your cum like you did me!"

"What?! You are out of your damn mind! Get OUT OF MY CAR!"

"Make me!"

Valley dove to the driver side of the car, and Ramses was right after her. Watching for her blade and her quick hand, Ramses grabbed Valley by the foot to drag her out, but she twisted around and lunged for him— blade first and screaming a warrior's call.

"Say you love me!" Valley screamed at the top of her lungs and stabbed her blade into his shoulder.

Ramses tried to get out of the way, but the blade of the pocket knife was black as night, and hard to see against the dark. Ramses fell out of the car, and landed on the ground with his back against the oak tree he'd parked by. He yelled in agony as the knife was still lodged within the wound.

Valley sat in the car and watched as Ramses slowly pulled the knife out of his shoulder. Blood slithered out of the opening, and the sight of it all thrilled her to no end. She got out of the car, and walked over to him. The loss of blood made him too tired to move out of her way.

"Say you'll never leave me." Valley bent over him and whispered those words in his ear as she straddled him. She kissed his lips seductively, and asked again. "Say you love me."

There was no response from Ramses. He looked away angrily; unable to remove the girl from his lap due to the deep gash rendering the arm useless. Valley took the knife from his shoulder, and thrust it into his side. Ramses winched in pain. Blood oozed out of his side wound and onto the cobblestone sidewalk. The sight of his own bodily secretion everywhere he looked made him dizzy.

Ramses squirmed under her weight. He wanted so desperately to get away, but he was too badly bruised to struggle any harder. The motion from his attempt to escape, and the way their pelvises were aligned excited her. Valley closed her eyes, and began to imagine that she was making love to him once again. She took her knife, and used it to slice open his shirt. As the blade ripped open his shirt open, it also made contact with his skin, opening up his chest in one clean cut to his navel— his body arched upwards underneath hers from the incision; writhing slowly from the pain. The pressure his movement created in her pleasurable space aroused her, and she began to move her body rhythmically along with his. She began grinding herself purposely; forcing her crotch into his... rubbing her private area against his; imagining his limp penis wanted to be inside of her.

Valley pressed her body harder on him while circling her hips slow then fast. She felt her flower bloom as she gyrated her hips around and around over top of his white denim jeans. As she continued to stimulate herself, Ramses moaned in deathly pain. Vocalizing his anguish only heightened Valley's yearning to be with him. "Yes Ramses. I want you too... I'm about to cum just for you, baby." Valley laid her torso on him, and as she felt herself climax inside her panties, she gave Ramses a soft kiss on his flushed cheek. "Did you like that, my love? Was I better this time? Was I better than her? Better than that slut Giselle? Do you love me now?"

"Please just leave me alone..." Ramses felt violated as he was forced to partake in such a demented display of lust and desire.

Valley sucked her teeth at his incessant whining, and then slapped him hard out of frustration. "Why Ramses… why continue to play these games? We just made love, our child is growing in my womb, and you STILL deny what you really feel for me!" Valley removed herself from his lap, angry that he still would not come back to her willingly.

"I love you. I love you so much that I can't let you go." Valley paced in front of him as she thought things through. "You are my reason to live, and yet, you choose to withhold your love so that I may die from the lack of it." Valley shook her head at his shameful denial of their true existence together. "Regretfully, I have to ask if you understand what has to happen."

"What is it that you want from me?!" Ramses watched her walk back in forth in front of him as he fearfully wondered about his fate.

"Just shut up! Shut up, and let me tell you what I want! Just be quiet a moment while I talk!" She stopped pacing and stared at him. He was beautiful, and almost close to being hers for the rest of her life. She teared up, and began to weep at the thought of them finally being together. "I just love you so much Ramses… but because you will not let me live my life standing beside you, you will have to live the rest of your life inside of me as we merge into one."

Valley sliced her arm once again and then placed the open wound onto Ramses' bleeding side letting their blood mix together. Ramses eyes rolled into the back of his head as he felt the pain of the gash she'd created being pressed open.

"There. Now you will always be inside of me for the rest of my life. Never ever to be with that whore that tore us apart." The pure thought of his blood running through her veins sent chills up her spine.

"I love you so much...." Valley placed the blade downward and over his chest, and with the quickest gesture... she forced the blade into his body where his heart lay. Blood gushed from his chest, flowing river red down his body. Ramses wanted to cry out, but instead, he gasped for air as his eyes bulged.

He struggled desperately to try and make some kind of noise... for someone to hear him other than the deranged woman that stood before him, but there were no words to utter... no sounds to express what he felt. "Shush." Valley saw his desperation and cupped a hand over his soft angelic lips to help him quiet his soul. "Shush, shush, my love. Don't try and talk." Valley took the knife from his heart, and brought it back down directly in the gaping chest wound. She twisted the knife slowly from left to right making sure to dig the blade deep within.

"No one will love you like I do, baby..." Valley pulled the knife out once again and wiped its drippings into her own incision. She kissed his cheek and continued kissing down his neck as she heard him take his last breaths.

For one brief moment, she thought she heard him whisper "why".

She answered, "Because our love is bigger than us." She held a kiss on his lips until there wasn't life left in him. "Your death was a sacrifice to keep our love alive. Thank you for doing this for us." Valley whispered the words softly in his ear as his head went limp to the left.

Lifting herself from his bloody carcass, Valley began to take a long look at her darling. What she saw wasn't what she'd seen in him before they officially consummated their union. The vibrant eyes she gazed into that faithful night when they first met were now empty vessels. The long wavy hair he kept neatly pulled in a ponytail was an unruly halo above his head. His plump lips no longer had the rosy tent she longed to kiss. Instead, they were covered in dry, ashed on saliva, and remnants of blood tinted the corners of his mouth. He wasn't her lover anymore. He was disfigured, he was a mess, he didn't belong to her. Screwing her face up in disgust at his unsightly appearance, Valley walked away from the vile scene of him lying dead in his own blood. The death he created was not allowed to spoil the rest of her lovely night.

"Only you, dear Valley, could make a man look like this. He was strong and handsome and now he looks pathetic. You've corrupted him forever."

"You should have never come for him. You've tainted one of the Beautiful Ones. You will pay for your transgressions for sure."

"Shut up! Shut up! Shut up! Shut up! This is none of your business!" Valley yanked her hair as she screamed at the voices, while she ran down the street to get away from their clamor.

CHAPTER Twenty-Two

October 18, 2012

Oh my goodness, John! It happened just like you said it would! Everyone else kept telling me that he didn't love me, that he doesn't want me, but I didn't listen! And now! We are together! John, it was such a magical night— just like in a fairytale! He waited for me after the party, he carried me to the car, and then John, we made love in the moonlight! It was all so very lovely and romantic. Once we finished, he vowed never to be with anyone else ever again, and we sealed our pact in blood. He's all mine now. I see our future together, and one day we will be married. Oh, and I think I'm pregnant.

Valley reached in her pocket and pulled out her trusty pocket knife. She then kissed it cheerfully; placing it in her journal before she closed its pages. Putting John back in his place in the furthest corner underneath the bed, Valley hopped in between the covers on the twin mattress; rolling over to face the wall for a good night's rest.

Unfortunately, rest was not so sound for Valley. The voices in her head she'd been trying to keep at bay rose in volume as she moved from one resting position to another. Closing her eyes also brought up the old terror of the monsters that watched her while she slept. These monsters weren't the ordinary kind that scared children in the dark with their hairy faces, sharp teeth, and googley eyes. These monsters didn't have a face, they didn't have a shape. They just watched her while she slept, and as she laid there with her eyes closed, they would get closer and closer, until she'd wake in a panic and drenched in sweat.

Not wanting the monsters to get her, Valley usually kept her eyes open and stayed very alert when they came. She would watch them watching her as they stuck their long sharp claws into the plastered walls climbing up to the ceilings to roam— stalking Valley in the dark. The monsters scared her. She feared them... not knowing what they wanted or why they were there. They made her heartbeat fast as they made deep hollow moans while they walked the ceilings and the walls, but as long as she kept her eyes on them, she knew they wouldn't get her. And just like every morning, the monsters slowly faded away. Safe from the fear as the dawn appeared, Valley was sure she would be able to catch a nap before her first class, just like she'd been doing every morning the monsters had returned to torment her.

Her eyelids finally closed as the sun started to peek over the horizon, but her early morning nap was interrupted by her roommate storming through the door, sobbing and blubbering about something Valley was unable to understand. Giselle reached for the television remote and changed the channel to the local breaking news.

"I can't even believe it's all true! I thought he was going to leave her!"

"...Yes, that's right Sabrina." The young woman's voice on the television caught Valley's attention as it drowned out Giselle's inaudible ranting. "The young man who has yet to be identified, was found in the Fan District brutally stabbed to death. Residence of The Fan did not hear anything unusual last night when the horrific murder occurred. His car was found here behind a line of trash cans in this alley. People living in this building behind me say there was a party going on a few blocks down, and believe that the young man may have been there."

The camera followed the newscaster back to where a young lady stood solemn with her head hanging low. "Standing here with me is Sherry Vaughn. Rocked by the loss of another senseless act of violence, Sherry has vowed to assist the police in any way she knows how to bring a sadistic killer to justice."

"The killings need to stop. I knew this young man personally and it is tragic that he is gone. The time has come for us to put down our weapons and make Richmond a better place. I will help the police in any way I know how to avenge his death."

The news reporter brought the mic back to her mouth to finish reporting. "So far, the police have not been able to find the murder weapon nor do they have any leads in a crime that has devastated the local community. This is Evelyn Braccus reporting live for Channel 12 news. Back to you Sabrina…"

"Valley! Look and see! It's the girl from the phone! She knows it was you who killed him! She's going to find you and hurt you!"

"Giselle knows who she is! Giselle knew about Sherry Vaughn! Giselle isn't your friend because she didn't tell you about her! We are your only friends!"

Valley looked at Giselle perplexed by what she witnessed on television, and why her friend would betray her and not tell her that Ramses was seeing someone else. "Who the fuck was that bitch with the news caster?"

"Huh… what bitch?"

"That bitch— the one who said she was going to help the police find his killer… she acts like she's in love with him or something."

Giselle wiped her nose; appalled that Valley was more interested in what was on television than why she was crying. "Seriously Valley? That's all you see— that a woman wants to find a killer?"

"They weren't just on there talking about finding a killer; they flaunted her all over the television like the whole thing was all about her! Tell me Giselle... did you know about her?"

"Of course I know her! Everyone does! I've met her several times, but what does that have to do with right now?!"

Valley got off the bed and slowly walked over to Giselle; looking at her in a chastising way. "So you mean to tell me you have been sneaking around having sex with a committed man?! How sick is that?! How sick are you?! That is the *nastiest*, vilest thing I could ever think of! How could you— someone who has been raised to be a respected woman, be involved in such a situation!" Valley put her hands on her hips and contorted her face in disgust.

The room grew silent after her last declaration. It was awkward for Giselle to have mention she was involved in a lover's tryst since Valley didn't know that side of her, but the cat was out of the bag, and she had to deal with the repercussions.

Giselle sucked her teeth nonchalantly at Valley's old style way of thinking. "Oh Valley, get off it. It wasn't like he didn't tell me he was going to leave her eventually. You act like you are so innocent and never make any mistakes." Giselle got off of the bed and made her way to her closet to find something to change into.

"Innocent is not the word I'm looking for... maybe what you're thinking is I'm not a SLUT like you!"

Giselle threw the shirt she had in her hand on the floor in outrage. "Slut?! Are you serious?! You are just jealous that I can get a man to look at me for more than two seconds without throwing up! You're just jealous that people like ME and want to be around ME, and they laugh at YOU!"

"I'm sorry, but you are mistakenly equating popularity and congeniality with SLUT! You are a SLUT, you've always been a SLUT, and you will always be a SLUT!"

"OOOH!" Giselle squealed, and turned back to the closet; furious at her friend for her very unkind remarks. "You know what Val, I've been carrying you for long enough! I've tried to bring you out of your little itty bitty shell, and change your awful serial killer look since the time we got here! If you haven't caught on, I've pitied you since I met you, but you have really crossed a line!"

Valley kept her arms folded, and her brow furrowed as she watched her former best friend pack her things. "Well, it's good to know how you really feel about me! All this time, I thought you actually liked me."

"No, Valley. All this time I was trying to use you for some reason or another." Giselle spat the words out sarcastically as she continued to grab her things. "You can do whatever you want to this side of the room. I'm not coming back." With those last words, Giselle was out of the room for good.

"Why did you let her leave! Now we have no one!"

"Let her go. We don't need her anymore. We have what we want. Ramses is ours forever."

"Settle down you two. We still have something unexpected to deal with." Valley stared at the closed door as a sinister smile crept onto her face. "We need to pay Sherry Vaughn a visit."

CHAPTER TWENTY-THREE

Early in the dawn of light, Valley sat on her ex-roommate's bed carving the name "Sherry" into her arm. The room was dim; lit by candles Valley had placed strategically on top of the dressers, in corners, and at the cracked opening of the closet free to express herself without the interruption of any distractions. Her reflection bounced and danced on the opposite wall, and she glanced at it from time to time, as if it were watching approvingly while she sealed her destiny.

"Sherry has to die."

"Sherry is a liar. She's the one who murdered him. We were the ones who saved him."

"Shut up! No one has to die! Ramses has paid his price for love! No more pain! No more suffering! No one else will die!"

"Sherry has to. She's the one who brings death. She's the one who should be dead."

"No! No death! Not anymore! Ramses is at peace! He's happy right here!" Valley placed her hand on her heart. She felt it pound harder than it ever had. "My heart beats strong. Ramses is with me!"

"No! He is dead! You killed him! You made him die because you only wanted him for yourself! It was you who murdered him!"

"Stop it! Stop it! Stop it! Stop it! Stop it! Stop it!" Valley banged her head with her fist annoyed by the way the voices double –talked, and twisted their words.

"It was you all along! It wasn't Sherry at all! You are the one who stabbed him until there was nothing left! It is all your fault!"

"It was Sherry! I saved him! Sherry killed him!"

Yes! It was Sherry! Kill Sherry for him! Kill Sherry for Us!"

Valley allowed her blood to run loose down her arm and stain Giselle's bed. She'd been cutting on her limbs for hours thinking on Sherry and the problems she'd caused. Listlessly, she removed herself from the soiled sheets feeling quite faint from all the blood she'd lost. It was agreed on what she must do to settle his score, and now she had to prepare.

The loss of blood was not the only thing affecting Valley's shift in moods. Her once anxious fever to be with Ramses was what fueled her reverence to life, but now that she had what she wanted, the energy to exist had now simmered to a low heat and she finally felt like she was coming to a slow crawl. Her limbs dragged on each side of her body unnaturally as she walked; swinging slowly back and forth. Her legs felt like dead logs she had to lift just to make progress down the dorm's hall.

Going for her shower, she kept her knife cradled in the curved palm of her hand. Big Black was being held in the other. Her eyes looked straight forward but focused on nothing; instinctively following the path she took every morning to the bathrooms. Her dorm mates watched the girl known as "The crazy bitch from the party the other night" make her way to the bathroom with her unusual choice of shower essentials and drastic scrapes up and down her legs and arms. Some laughed. Others pointed. Valley didn't care.

She eventually found herself at the back shower stall with the hot water steaming her in. She stood under the falling stream cleansing her cut arms. She had already loosened her grip on her blade which had now dropped onto the ceramic floor with a *"CLANK!"*

Rubbing one hand all over her wet body, Valley grazed her nipples unbeknownst to her own consciousness. *"I feel you touch me Ramses…"* Her fingers pinched her pink raised nubs in between each other; becoming aroused by her own hand. Big Black strolled down her leg resting at her private entrance.

"No… Ramses. Not now."

Big Black let his tip touch her red haired unshaven lips.

"No. You were just with her. I saw her on television talking about you."

Not the one to take "no" for an answer, Big Black finally forced his way in between her thighs and into her opening.

"Ouch! I said 'no'!"

Her dildo began to thrust itself in and out, back and forth. Valley screamed out in pain as he had his way with her.

"Ramses! Stop it! Stop it! I can't take you hurting me!" Valley's hand moved faster and faster manipulating Big Black as he delivered pain and shock to her nether region.

Valley pinched her nipples harder turning them from a soft fleshy shade of pink to a blood red. With the assistance of her hand, Big Black pumped his shaft harder and harder; jamming himself in and out retrieving streams of blood as he retracted.

The commotion of Valley's action caused a scene. Her dorm mate's crowded around the shower assuming from the loud screams and moans, that someone was being assaulted. What they found was Valley in full masturbatory agony. They heard her cries, but were confused as to why she pleaded the way she did.

"This bitch is nuts! Someone go in there and tell her she's by herself!"

"I'm not doing it! Don't you see that blade on the floor! She probably got another one under her tongue!"

"Well... someone needs to shake that bitch coherent! She has lost her damn mind!"

CHAPTER TWENTY-FOUR

The time has come for the end.
The end of life.
The end of death.
The end of all.

Time.
Time will stop life.
Time will cease death.
The end of her time will be her death.
Her death will happen for the death she created.

No longer existing.
Nothing to tell.
Sherry will die
In time.

Valley's ode to Sherry took all of the morning to carve into the painted cement wall across the street from the university's campus. The blade of her pocket knife had become dull from scratching and digging into the old chewed up walls, but the poem she wrote to commemorate the moment was perfectly magnificent. In the dank and darkness of the excavated room, Valley sat Indian-style in front of her work, marveling at how the words pierced the crumbling edifice... the letters flowing across it in an imperfect fashion. Adding to the poems depth, Valley wrote "Sherry" in big letters, little letters, slanted up, and slanted down all over the walls that surrounded her; decorating and intensifying the poem's ramification.

"Perfect." She announced out loud in the dark shelled out building. Her masterpiece distracted her from the reality she ignored. She sat and watched the walls hoping the words would jump off of the flat surface and make her take action against the enemy.

"It's time for you to complete your mission."

"Yes, you have set the plan in motion. The time is now. You have to find her and kill what's left of his bad habit."

"You're right. He put this on me to do, and I must finish so that we can finally be together in peace."

Getting up from her spot on the cold wet floor, Valley walked slowly towards the wall, touching the tortured words symbolically, and then headed back towards her dorm.

The plan for Sherry's death came to Valley in a dream. The voices in her head that shouted their opinions constantly helped Valley devise a sinister plot to eliminate her most hated foe. The voices were very critical, and usually their message was jumbled inside of her brain, but they were very clear about what needed to happen with Sherry Vaughn. In previous talks, the most the voices had ever told her to do was mark her own body with scars and scratches to remind herself of her failures. They preferred Valley to use a knife on her alabaster skin— it satisfied their need to hear the long moan of pain as the knife slid down her limbs, but for the duty of killing Sherry Vaughn, they wanted her gone immediately.

Their instructions for Valley were to get a can of gasoline and a match to light Sherry Vaughn on fire. The stench of her burned flesh permeating the air would really make the voices proud. First, Valley had to find the treacherous man-stealer before they could make her burn in hell. That part of the plan was going to be hard considering Valley didn't have any inclination as to where she should start her journey to find her target. On the voices insistence, there wasn't much time to find and kill Sherry Vaughn. They needed to fill their taste for revenge for Sherry's transgression. They were impatient, and the longer it took to kill Sherry, the more assertive they became with Valley. The consequences for Valley not following through were dire. If she didn't follow their directive, they would punish her with self mutilation. If she took longer than they expected to fulfill their desire, they would haunt her dreams and her thoughts never ceasing for the rest of her days. It was clear the decision to kill Sherry was not hers to make. The voices had proven they were stronger than her own will.

In deep thought about the plan, Valley walked across the street focused on getting back to her dorm room. She didn't even think to look where she was going which caused two cars to swerve into each other; both trying not to hit the pale red head aimlessly walking right into their path.

Valley continued onward to her room— pushing through the dense crowd that had assembled on the University's front yard. Valley didn't care about them. She had to get to her room because she hadn't told John about her new mission and he was always the first to know.

Trying to pass through the mass of people that was standing around was a struggle. Valley pushed and jabbed the group to get through them. The people around her took her assertiveness as unneeded aggression and made It even more difficult for her to find her way.

Soon, the crowd was yelling and clapping. They were pushing her around with their bodies, yelling, clapping, and shouting. Valley didn't want any part of it. She just wanted to get to her room to finalize her plans.

"And now, I would like to introduce a phenomenal woman. A woman who has done so much for her cause. Sherry Vaughn, could you please come to the stage!"

The crowd began to clap and shout once again. Valley hated the loud noise and retreated downward; squatting and folding her lanky body into an orb in the midst of the crowd.

"Shut the noise up! Shut the noise up! Stop clapping! I can't take the clapping!" With the noise from the crowd and her vocal pleas for the voices inside her head and out to cease their infernal racket, Valley almost didn't hear the object of her fixation, Sherry Vaughn, being called to the stage.

Valley rose from her position on the ground in awe of her target taking her place behind the podium. She couldn't believe fate had finally bought the two of them together.

"It's her! Don't waste this moment! Kill her now!"

"I can't! I don't have the gasoline or the match!" Valley arguably whispered to herself.

"Do it now or we will never stop telling you! We will never stop telling you!"

"Shut up! Shut up! Shut up! Shut up!" Valley banged her fists against her head in irritation— trying to figure out how she could pull off her kill without the materials for the fire. Then she felt in her possession the dulled knife she'd used when carving her poem into the cement and plaster wall of the building across the street.

"This will have to do." Valley thought to herself.

CHAPTER TWENTY-FIVE

"Thank you Union University for inviting me here today. We have come a long way, but we still continue to struggle with the violence around us— this corridor especially. Union... a place where young minds are molded and developed, sits right in the midst of drugs on one end and violence at another. Students, with your help, we can stop the danger! We can stop the crime! We can stop the violence!"

As the crowd clapped for the rousing sentiments, Valley rushed the stage like a vigilante. With her warrior's cry loud and empowering, Valley lunged for Sherry with a vengeful strike.

Leaping for her opponent, Valley tackled Sherry with her back headed for the floor. "You tried to take him from me! You tried to make people believe you loved him more than I do!"

"Someone help me!" Scared for her life, Sherry struggled to keep her assailant at bay with just her own limbs between them.

"Look at her yelling for her life! Kill her now! Stab the knife between her eyes! Do it now!"

Valley tried her best to force the blade closer to Sherry's face, but she wasn't strong enough to penetrate her victim's shield.

"Help me please! Someone please help me kill her! She's a murderer!" Valley cried out for assistance with finishing Sherry's death, but the crowd just looked on in shock.

Continuing her battle, Valley saw an opening where she could put the blade in Sherry's chest. Just as she was about to make the plunge, she was pulled away by onlookers that had finally decided to act on Sherry's pleas for mercy.

"What are they doing?! They have stopped you from freeing us! Tell them she is the one who needs to be stopped!"

"Get off me! I have to kill her! She's the enemy! Why are you helping her?! She's a murderer! She's killed my boyfriend! Someone stop her!" Valley unsuccessfully wrestled with her detainers; trying her best to get away from their grasp. She was shocked to see others brushing Sherry off, and making sure she was not harmed in the whole ordeal. Sherry was even helpfully escorted to the back of the stage to be checked out by the medics.

"Ma'am…. Could you please calm down and tell us why you attacked Mrs. Sherry Vaughn?"

Valley looked at the policeman standing in front of her. He had his note pad out ready to take the details of the altercation while his partner briefed the station on what they both just witnessed.

"Sherry is a murderer! Doesn't anyone hear me?! She brutally killed my fiancé, and she stands before you talking about stopping the violence! She needs to be apprehended for her crimes! Arrest her now!"

"Congresswoman Vaughn is no killer, Miss. She came here today to speak at the 'Stop the Violence Rally'. She's a respected member of the community. Sorry to inform you but you have a case of mistaken identity." The policeman wrote down some of the things Valley said on his pad as he talked to her— all while smacking on a piece of spearmint gum.

"No! She's the one! She's the one who killed my fiancé in cold blood! She's killed the father of my unborn child!"

"Frank, call it in and see what you can find out about this murder she's talking about." The policeman taking notes hollered the orders over his shoulder at his partner for confirmation of Valley's story.

"Listen ma'am, I can't see Congresswoman Vaughn committing a crime like that. She's a nice lady who's loved and respected around here. Until we work this out, I want you to come with me." The policeman pulled out his handcuffs and the crank of the lock from them startled her into another altered rendition of her actions.

"What are those for?! Why am I being arrested?! Please don't arrest me!" Valley's voice went into a panicked whine as she pleaded with the nonchalant officer.

"I'm not arresting you. I just want to put these on you for my safety and yours. You did, in fact, tackle someone, and you're carrying a weapon." The policeman yanked the blade from Valley, and then placed the cuffs on her; gently grabbing her arm and escorting her to the squad car.

"Duck your head, Miss…"

Valley sat in the backseat of the police car, dumbfounded as to what was going on. She turned around to see where she'd come from. The banner over the stage showed that she was just at a National Night Out. Since the commotion she caused was now cleared and mostly forgotten, people were back to listening to the music being played by the DJ. Some were eating free food provided by the vendors, and others were engaged in field games and pony rides.

The backseat police car side window was rolled up half the way. She heard when the policeman reported back that there wasn't a murder that fit the description Valley gave them. Both cops looked at her with question in their eyes. Neither one could make out what the strange woman's reasons for attacking the congresswoman.

"Officer, I heard about all of the commotion and wanted to check things out."

Valley looked up from within the squad car to see Giselle standing there.

"Giz! Giz! Giz! Giz!" Valley yelled out of the window in hopes of getting Giselle's attention, but Giselle turned and looked at her pathetically and smiled in acknowledgement.

"My name is Giselle. I'm with the Student Government Group here at Union. I put the National Night Out Rally together this year, and I heard our congresswoman was attacked by this young lady."

"Yeah. Do you know her? She says the congresswoman attacked her boyfriend and that's why she came at her with the knife."

Giselle looked over at Valley inside of the car. *"Pathetic."* She thought to herself. She shook her head in disappointment, and turned her conversation back to the police officer. "Well, I thought I knew her, but it turns out I didn't know too much about her at all, officer. We used to be best friends until she spazzed out on me a couple of days ago."

"So she's enrolled at Union?"

"Yeah. You could say that, but she hasn't been to classes in weeks, and I believe she's been hanging out in that building across the street instead of going to classes like she says she's been doing.

"The abandoned one?" The police officer nodded his head to the building that stood alone in a vacant field that was littered with trash and debris.

"Yes. I see her come out of there from time to time." I think it's weird she goes there so much.

The police stared at the abandoned building trying to get an idea as to why anyone would want to entertain their selves there. It showed years of wear and tear. No window panes and the bricks appeared to be crumbling as minutes of the day clicked by.

"Like I said, up until a couple of days ago, we were the best of friends, and did everything together. Lately though, she's been very hostile towards me and acting really creepy. She finally flipped out on me one day when I came to the room to tell her about the horrible breakup I just had with my boyfriend. I think she believes I was cheating with him— she kept talking about me being a slut and sleeping around, but honestly, he was the one cheating on me!"

"Hold on ma'am. Let's stick to one subject here." The officer put his hands up to slow Giselle down and to focus her back on the real issue. "I know a breakup can be a horrible thing, but let's focus on your friend here."

"Sorry Mr. Officer. I just get emotional when I think about that scum bag." Giselle folded her arms and thought about her ex boyfriend for a moment before she continued. "Well anyway, after that, I just moved out. I should have known then something was wrong with her. She's never been this crazy before even though the little nut bag has done some off-the-wall shit when we were younger."

A slew of past incidents flooded her memory when she mentioned that tidbit of information to the police. She began to chuckle at the memories. "The craziest thing she's ever done though was show up bald headed to her dad's funeral with some fake poison! It was the wildest thing I'd ever seen! I thought she was fucking with her mom's, and trying to embarrass her." Speaking the truth about Valley's actions put everything in a different perspective for Giselle and the laughter ceased. She lowered her head in shame; embarrassed that she hadn't noticed that her friend had a problem for such a long time.

Giselle's face grew solemn and she looked back at Valley who was staring back at her like a doe-eyed deer. Giselle waved sympathetically at her, but Valley didn't wave back; her stare drifted upwards and stayed fixated on the police car's ceiling. She turned her focus back to the cop more introspective about the whole ordeal. "I know now I should have talked to our counselor about her erratic behavior and maybe none of this would have happened."

"Don't blame yourself, Miss. Sometimes you just can't see when someone is off their rocker until it's too late. Your testimony has been helpful. I'll take her down to the precinct and see what the city will do for her."

CHAPTER TWENTY-SIX

Dr. Sumpter sat at his desk for the last time. His residency at Central State was finally over. He'd already boxed up his things and the walls where he'd displayed family pictures and his many degrees and certificates were finally bare. His oak desk was occupied with just his laptop and his faithful tape recorder. Leaving this office symbolized the last time he would write about his "project", or better known to the world as Valley Rain De'Amore.

Ashamed of what he'd done to Valley— how he studied her for so many years without interfering; knowing at times he should have interceded when it came to her well being was without question the wrong thing to do. He wasn't ethical. His greed made him an animal searching for fame. He used her for his own personal gain, and she was the one who paid the price. Her mental state had deteriorated tremendously since she entered Central State because of his own actions. He should have put her on the right regime of medication as soon as he became her therapist, but he chose to see what raw emotions he could bring out of her. Feeling he was so close to having that breakthrough moment which would have changed both of their lives forever fueled the illogical choice to keep her "wild". Not administering those meds earlier on was the worst decision he ever made. Mentally, she was now too far gone for any pill to bring her back. No drug available would be strong enough to assist in her having a coherent thought about anything. This was a sad day for Dr.

Sumpter. It was now time for him to step aside and allow his patient to get real, unbiased professional assistance. All-in-all... he had failed.

At three o'clock, the new doctor assigned to her case would meet him in the main lobby. He gathered the rest of his things off of his desk, and made his way down the badly lit hall. As he approached Valley's door, he saw a young woman standing in front of it, watching his patient through the door's window pane. The young lady turned in time to see him approach.

"Doctor Sumpter?"

"Yes..."

"I'm Doctor Star Alexandria, and I'll be taking over your patient, Valley Rain De'Amore's case." She smiled stiffly at him— unmoved to meet the "great" Dr. Sumpter

Dr. Sumpter stuck out his hand to shake hers; happy to greet the petite doctor on his way out, and to put the whole Valley debacle in the past.

"It's nice to meet you, but weren't we supposed to meet in the lobby?" Dr. Sumpter looked at her slightly confused as to why she didn't wait for him where they had agreed upon.

"We were. I'm very familiar with this hospital as I have treated patients here before. I felt the need to observe my newest patient, Valley before your briefing." Dr. Alexandria turned her attention back to Valley who sat in quiet and calm, and staring blankly back at them. Not taking her attention off of Valley, she continued her conversation with the doctor. "I've received the copy you sent me of her case." Dr. Alexandria stated frankly. "I found it a quite interesting read." She paused her sentence before she continued. "What I found the most interesting was that you've been her doctor since she was in foster care?"

"That is correct. I have been watching over Valley for many years. I met her when she was around five or six. I learned then that a transient couple found her in a drainage pipe by the side of the road; her mother dead with a needle in her arm lay beside her. In my hypothesis, I believe her troubles started there with the untimely death of her mother, and the unknown whereabouts of her father." Dr. Sumpter nodded matter-of-factly before he continued.

"In the early years, my goal with Valley's treatment was to recover those premature memories... to find that instant where all her troubles began. I do believe that it was there, in that drainage pipe, a monster was born." Dr. Sumpter spoke proudly of his theory, but he could tell Dr. Alexandria was not impressed with his pompous arrogance or by calling a human being a "monster".

Uninterested in Dr. Sumpter and his theories, she continued the conversation to gather the information required to start her patient's treatment over. "So she's had a hard start at life I see..."

"Unfortunately, I'm afraid so. Her adoptive parents tried to make a go of it, and their care seemed to do her some good. However, I believe the death of her adoptive father triggered something inside of her that has haunted her psyche for a very long time. And now, it's regrettably manifested into an extreme case of schizophrenia."

"I see." Dr. Alexandria said in a sing-song voice.

Valley slowly got up from the floor and walked zombie-like to the door and stood in front of them... still staring blankly in their direction... as if they weren't there discussing her mental stability. Her hair was disheveled, her face healing from multiple scratches; Dr. Alexandria jotted notes down about the sudden change in movement from her patient. She tapped on Valley's window in hopes that she would respond, but she didn't acknowledge them. She looked through them both, only twitching her head in one direction or another to hear something distant and far off.

"How is her mental state now, Dr. Sumpter?"

"It's worsening. As you can tell she isn't fairing well behind these walls. I believe her new condition is bought on by the new regimen of pills I have put her on. You may find the medication of no use, but she was at the point of being uncontrollable. This set of medication has calmed her down tremendously." The truth was the pills were of no consequence now. Valley's change was brought on by time and a declining will to fight off psychosis, but not because of the new pills she was taking. In front of Dr. Alexandria, Dr. Sumpter tried to redeem himself by mentioning the medication he'd placed her on. He was ashamed to have someone see how poor of a job he'd done with Valley.

Dr. Alexandria continued her briefing— feeling the uneasiness Dr. Sumpter was trying so hard to hide. "In her file, she reports that someone killed her boyfriend, and she attacked the killer."

"Yes, this is the problem we've been having since she was admitted here. From what I can tell, she's always had destructive tendencies but has kept them repressed for some reason or another. Before she left for college, she believed her mother had her father killed for a treasure she claims was hidden in the basement. We found this piece of information out through her diary that was dropped off by her mother on her last visit to see her daughter. Valley's mother reported, and it has been verified in Valley's journal she's named John, that Valley was paranoid that she was next to die by her mother's hands."

Dr. Alexandria jotted down more notes before she continued her questions. "Did she show any symptoms of schizophrenia before her last outburst?"

"She's always had antisocial behavior. Why, I remember when she was younger and there were reports of her cutting a classmate's arm because she thought an alien bug was eating his insides."

"I did see something about that in her files..." Dr. Alexandria put her notepad away having received enough preemptive information.

Valley stood in their peripheral vision behind her closed door... almost listening to how Doctor Sumpter spoke of her. Dr. Alexandria listened as well. Her glaring look made him feel uncomfortable. He shifted his feet not able to look away from the absoluteness she foretold in her unwelcoming eyes.

She folded her arms as she continued. "So what about the boyfriend? Is he in fact dead?"

"No. There actually wasn't a boyfriend. There wasn't even a murder. The guy she referenced was actually a friend of a friend... I believe Giselle's friend if I've remembered correctly. The authorities and I have spoken to him about the night in question... where she says he died by the hands of Sherry Vaughn. He remembers seeing her at the party and he actually volunteered to take her home because she was clearly intoxicated, but she tried to stab him with a knife as he placed her in the car. He dodged the assault, but she fell out of the car, knocking her head against the sidewalk when she tried to attack him. She passed out from the blow, and he drove away; leaving her there."

"How dreadful." Dr. Alexandria shook her head at such misfortune. Valley put her hand against the small viewing window on the door. A slow smile came to her face, but her eyes remained vacant. Suddenly a high pitched giggle came from her lips.

Trying to ignore Valley's behavior, Dr. Alexandria began her questioning once more. "You haven't been able to get her to recognize that what she experienced this whole time was imagined? That her thoughts have been hallucinations?"

Dr. Sumpter nodded in agreement. "Correct. She's so far in her own thoughts, she actually believes this tragedy happened."

"And her friend, Giselle?"

"Yes, Giselle came to my office one time before. She explained to me that Valley started to slowly lose her mind not too long after they got there. She said Valley began to isolate herself from the world. Often times making up stories about dating and having new friends to hang out with."

Doctor Sumpter fumbled through the notes looking for confirmation that Giselle's statement was in Valley's psychiatric file for future review. Confirming their existence, Dr. Sumpter proceeded. "It's all here in the notes I've added to her file for your review."

Dr. Alexandria nodded her head in understanding but never took her eyes off of Dr. Sumpter. She studied him as he summed up Valley's case for her.

"Doctor Sumpter. I've followed your work for many years. I've read your journals about the patient's you've had under your care. You have the tendency to take on cases that other doctors are reluctant to touch. I must say Doctor Sumpter, I find your methods of treatment highly questionable and border on being a mockery to this profession."

More angry than shocked, Dr. Sumpter huffed up his chest, and began to speak. "Doctor Alexandria. I beg your pardon, but your opinion about the treatment of my patients is not needed! I'm an accomplished Doctor who stands by my work, and my methods of treatment have been approved by higher levels of council. I don't need to tell you that I have also had a high percentage of success when it comes to curing my clients!"

"Yes… your success rate comes at a hefty price for your patients, and unfortunately for this poor young lady, she had to bear the brunt of your precarious methods. Let me make you aware that I have spoken to several boards about your methods of treatments, and have called for an investigation on your treatment process." Dr. Alexandria pulled out of her briefcase a white envelope and handed it to Dr. Sumpter. "This is a summary of what I have brought to the boards attention in regards to your treatment. Please feel free to peruse it, but you will find that all of my accusations are founded." Dr. Sumpter looked at Dr. Alexandria in shock and unable to dispute her claims because he knew most of them were probably true.

With her other hand, Dr. Alexandria shook Dr. Sumpters. She took one more look at Valley who still stood at the window giggling incessantly, and began to walk away. "Goodbye Dr. Sumpter. I hope to accomplish what you couldn't, and that is to break the mental barriers that you have reinforced."